MR. DARCY'S MISSING BRIDE

POWER OF DARCY'S LOVE - BOOK 1

VIOLET KING

PEMBERLEY PLAYGROUND PRESS

Compromised. Abducted. Rescued?

What if Elizabeth and Mr. Darcy met not at Hertfordshire but Hunsford? Rather than unwitting insults, they court in secret while exploring the grounds. It is perfect until the couple is caught in a compromising position. Will a forced engagement and a missing bride-to-be derail their love?

Find out in Mr. Darcy's Missing Bride, Book 1 of the Power of Darcy's Love series. Mr. Darcy's Missing Bride is a sweet, suspenseful romance of 30,000 words with a guaranteed happy ending.

If you love Pride and Prejudice Variations, start reading Mr. Darcy's Missing Bride today!

PROLOGUE

Thirst. Elizabeth thought she had never truly been thirsty before. Before, drinking happened without a second thought; a servant was called, and Elizabeth drank. Now, her tongue lay like dry dough in her mouth. Elizabeth ran her fingers along the damp, stone floor. Her chained leg clinked with her movement. The links ran to an iron ring nailed into the wall, too dark and too far away to see.

Elizabeth shivered.

Piles of root vegetables hunkered in the surrounding darkness, mostly potatoes and carrots. Between them scurried things which she preferred not know. A sip of plain water would be heaven sent, and the desire to stop the discomfort of being without dominated her thinking.

Light footsteps sounded above, interrupting the long silence.

"Please," Elizabeth rasped. She cleared her throat and spoke more loudly, "I need some water, please." The footsteps stopped, and she knew the owner of those soft footfalls was listening. "I am so thirsty."

"I am not allowed to open the cellar door," came a small voice. It was the boy, Aldous, Algon, Alfred – what was his name?

"I am really thirsty," she said, crawling to the base of the wooden ladder that led topside. She stood, reaching up to the trapdoor above. The chain pulled at her ankle. From above, a half-moon of light shone through a barred square hole in the trap door, revealing the shadowed outline of his cheek. "Will you give me some water?" Elizabeth asked.

Perhaps, he would open the door and climb down. It was a wild hope; the boy was too small to pull up the heavy, wooden door that led down into the cellar. He was only four or five from what she recalled. She heard him walk away and her hopes sank.

"Wait, please!" she cried, scratching at the ladder rung above her. "I am so thirsty, please." There was silence, then his footsteps returned.

"I can pour water through the bars," he said, his voice closer. "You will have to catch it."

"All right," she replied. She was willing to try anything. It was odd that the boy would think of something like that. He was just a boy, but maybe this wasn't the first time he had done this.

"Ready?" he asked.

"Yes," she replied. Who cared how he had figured out how to get water into the root cellar. He could be a child genius, or maybe someone had taught him. Either way, he was the holder of the water she desperately needed, and his idea was better than sitting in defeat.

The water dribbled down. She put her mouth up and caught some water, gulping and swallowing gratefully.

"More," she begged. It might sound unbecoming, but propriety was the farthest thing from her consciousness at this point. When Elizabeth had tried to escape, which landed her in this literal hell-hole, she never thought she'd be begging from a little boy who sounded as frightened as she. More water dribbled down through the opening.

Elizabeth heard a door open and held her breath. She heard a woman whispering, and the water stopped. "You will get us beat again," the woman hissed above.

"She be terrible thirsty, Mama," the boy said. "She will not be any good if she dies down there."

"He will put us both down there with her, if you get caught."

"It is not his fault," Elizabeth spoke up in the boy's defense. "I begged him for water. I am so thirsty."

"You should not have run, missy," the woman said. "That just made Bart angry."

"I know. I am sorry for that," Elizabeth said. There was silence, and she hoped she had not lost the woman. "Please, Willow."

After what seemed an interminable amount of time, she heard the latch click on the cellar door, and it lifted.

"Quick, give her the cup," the woman instructed the boy. He handed the cup down to Elizabeth. "Drink quick or we are all in trouble." She also handed her a bit of bread and meat.

Elizabeth gulped down the water. "Thank you," she gasped, giving the cup back to the boy. "Call me Lizzy," she said. Willow looked at her for a moment, then shook her head in the affirmative. Lizzy realized looking at Willow how thin she was, as was her son, compared to the girth her husband carried.

"I will try to get you more later," Willow said, her gaze sad. "I cannot promise, but I will try."

"Thank you," Elizabeth said trying to smile. Not that Willow would see. Still, the effort mattered.

Willow closed the door without replying. After a pause, when Elizabeth thought all was lost, the woman whispered, "If I get the chance, I will help you. No promises."

Then, they both left, and Elizabeth was alone in the dark, damp cellar. She had eaten a raw potato the night before and figured she could stomach another one. It was better than starving, but her stomach growled and twisted from both fright and the raw vegetables, to which she was unaccustomed.

The woman – Willow – had offered her water, bread and meat. Maybe Elizabeth could convince Willow to help her escape.

It was a wild bit of optimism, but Elizabeth hoped. Hope was all she had; hope, and the irrational dream Fitzwilliam Darcy would somehow find her in this place and rescue her.

CHAPTER 1

SOME WEEKS EARLIER

It was early morning, and the sun was resplendent, its rays coloring the budding floral displays and grasslands that appointed the gardens of Rosings. Elizabeth Bennet delighted in the patches of warm sunlight on her skin. It was the edge of summer, the end of spring and the weather was at its best: not too hot or cold, but warmth touching the earth and encouraging the flowers to bloom.

"Your husband speaks incessantly of Lady Catherine's nephew and his impending arrival." Elizabeth said as she walked with her friend Charlotte. Miss Maria Lucas, Charlotte's sister, had chosen to stay close to home that afternoon, pleading a headache, though Elizabeth suspected the young woman preferred to stay closer to the parsonage with her paints and small canvasses. Maria Lucas enjoyed drawing and painting and was talented at both.

Charlotte sighed. "Yes, William waxes poetic at the prospect of seeing Mr. Darcy, does he not? One might assume a long acquaintanceship from his words, but knowing William as I do, I am assured the praise is due wholly to Mr. Darcy's relation to the great Lady Catherine de Bourgh."

"Everything your husband praises has ties to Lady Catherine's thoughts, thus her good opinion gives him cause to enumerate all of Mr. Darcy's abundant virtues. As he does." Elizabeth could talk to Charlotte freely. They both knew her husband's nature. "Have you met Mr. Darcy?"

"No," Charlotte responded. "However, my husband has spoken paeans on Mr. Darcy's behalf. He finds him more than simply praiseworthy, but looks upon him with a level of adoration that I find hard to believe."

"Anyone who warrants that much approbation from your husband, who is only that fulsome in his praise of Lady Catherine, gives me pause."

"In what way, Lizzy?" Charlotte asked as they turned onto another path.

"I feel that too much praise of one person limits the reality of that person with faults, as we all have, and that person might think too much of themselves if no one gives them a realistic assessment."

"I would not prejudge," Charlotte responded.

"It is not a prejudgment, just my observation of human nature. Given nothing but praise, a person can believe themselves more than what they are, and their actions become reflective of that belief,"

"My husband can exaggerate a person's good qualities, and this opinion is coming from Lady Catherine."

"Yes, and Lady Catherine is not a person to overrate anyone who comes into her orbit."

Both women laughed at the thought of Lady Catherine finding anyone more than just tolerable.

Elizabeth continued, "The idea that Lady Catherine speaks so highly of Mr. Darcy would lead one to believe that he is exemplary in all that he does. Perfection comes with pride, and that can lead to being aloof and condescending with people."

"I do not believe that to be the case. And, even if I did, dear Lizzy, I would prefer to give Mr. Darcy the chance to prove his worldview before making any judgment."

"I am not prejudging him but merely stating precedent based upon my limited human observation."

"At least meet the man before deciding him an aloof boor, too full of himself by half to live in the world."

Both women laughed, continuing to walk together in the meadow. "Dear Heavens, Charlotte, I will not be rude with the man. I will give him a chance, but do not be surprised if he turns out to be a self-absorbed lout not worth the time we give him."

"Do not prejudge," Charlotte insisted again.

"I am not. For Heaven's sake, I have not laid eyes on the man, just heard your husband prattle on. He waited by the roadside and bowed as Mr. Darcy's carriage passed?"

Charlotte giggled. "Well, that is why we are out walking. I had to stop you chortling in his presence. How long do you think it would take for him to figure out you were laughing at and not with him? William sometimes takes things a bit far."

"On that point, I will not argue with you."

Their conversation was interrupted by the sound of horse hooves.

Confusion gave way to curiosity as two men on horseback rode perilously close, across the meadow and down the path.

Elizabeth backed away, stumbling.

"Lizzy!" Charlotte grabbed her arm.

The horses slowed.

"Miss, are you well?" A fair-haired man dismounted, releasing the reins of his horse and jogging to Elizabeth's side. He had a muscular build and bright, blue eyes.

"Well. I am well." Elizabeth took a breath, steadying herself.

The second man, dark-haired with a slimmer mien, dismounted. "Richard, we have disturbed these ladies enough."

"Hardly a disturbance," Charlotte said with a smile.

Annoyance flashed over the dark-haired man's expression before he schooled it to rigid formality. Both men bowed.

The fair-haired man said, "I am Colonel Richard Fitzwilliam, and this is my cousin and a great friend, Mr. Fitzwilliam Darcy."

Mr. Darcy bowed straight from the waist which

brought an involuntary smile to Elizabeth's lips. Stiff and aloof as expected.

Colonel Fitzwilliam continued, smiling: "And, to whom do we have the pleasure of speaking?" Elizabeth found him attractive, a shock of blond hair and blue eyes that seemed to twinkle in the sun. His partner said nothing, his dark gaze unreadable. Reserved might be a better term. *You are prejudging, Lizzy.*

Charlotte made introductions in return, making clear her married and Elizabeth's unmarried state, thus emphasizing her role as chaperone. Propriety maintained, each of them smiled awkwardly, waiting for someone to continue the conversation. Charlotte leaped into the pregnant pause, "I believe we will have dinner with you gentlemen this evening at your aunt's request."

"I see," Colonel Fitzwilliam replied. "That will be most pleasant, and we can get to know each other better."

"Yes, I am looking forward to spending another evening with your aunt." Colonel Fitzwilliam laughed, and Elizabeth noted with curiosity, Mr. Darcy's reaction. It was subtle, but there was a quirk in his lips that reached his eyes. Humor? She thought him distant, that touch of mirth tugged at her consciousness.

"Miss Bennet, I am glad you will grace us with your presence. It will make the evening that much merrier, I suspect." He offered his hand which Elizabeth took and started walking. Mr. Darcy and Charlotte fell in behind, leading the horses alongside.

"I am sure I cannot wait for that occasion. I so enjoyed having dinner with her a week past. It was indeed memorable."

Elizabeth smiled as she spoke. In actuality, it had been quite trying with Lady Catherine giving unwanted advice from the price of livestock to the marrying within your class. Each of these missives had been delivered with Mr. Collins agreeing on every point.

Miss Maria Lucas had barely spoken three words, and it seemed she'd like to hide herself under the table as she focused on her meal with grim determination.

"Your sister is very modest," Lady Catherine said. "A fine trait in any lady, and Mr. Collins has shown me some of her sketches. Very emotive. The style is still lacking, but with more practice and a dedicated tutor, Miss Maria may, perhaps, gain some accomplishment."

"I find her drawings very fine," Elizabeth said.

"Yes, you certainly would. Miss Lucas, I will give Mr. Collins the addresses of some fine tutors. I was once proclaimed quite talented, though my eyesight has begun to fail."

"Oh, Lady Catherine, do not jest!" Mr. Collins interjected. "Why, your eyes are as young as a spring bird's, just cracked from its shell. Why, you noted the uneven curtains on our second floor as you passed by our parsonage just last month, and explained not only the nature of the problem but offered many excellent solutions, is that not right, Charlotte?"

"Very right," Charlotte said, spearing meat with her fork. "We took every suggestion to heart, as always."

"As you ought! Miss Maria, you will be pleased for lessons three times weekly, will that suffice?"

Miss Maria looked up, her face pink. "Umm...as you wish, Lady Catherine," she mumbled.

"Yes, very modest, indeed," Lady Catherine said. Her gaze flitted to Elizabeth and narrowed.

The entire affair had given Elizabeth a headache and a jaw ache from smiling so much. At least, the food was well prepared and the wine refreshing. Elizabeth could better take all the advice with a bit of wine to offset the delivery.

"We are looking forward to an evening with our aunt, are we not, Darcy?" Colonel Fitzwilliam turned in his friend's direction slowing his pace.

"Yes, it is something I look forward to with every visit."

"She thinks the world of Mr. Darcy, and tells us always that he is simultaneously a paragon of virtue, a white knight and the most intelligent gentleman in all of Derbyshire."

"And what of you, Colonel Fitzwilliam? Surely, Lady Catherine thinks just as highly of you," Elizabeth replied, looking at him squarely. "A military man of your rank and status, she must have wonderful things to say."

"I am but a poor relation compared to Mr. Darcy. I am, however, the more congenial of the two of us. My dear friend, Mr. Darcy, judges everyone from that pedestal he lives on."

Pedestal? Maybe, she had been right to prejudge him after all.

"You jest, dear Richard." Darcy replied quietly. "I do not live on a pedestal, at least not a very large one. And, only my aunt thinks I'm a paragon of virtue."

Everyone looked at Mr. Darcy for a moment, then broke into laughter. "Good one, Darcy." Colonel Fitzwilliam replied. "We are best of friends, you know."

"I can see," Charlotte smiled.

"So, would you say then that your angel wings are singed about the edges?" It fell out of Elizabeth's mouth before she thought about the implications of her statement. It was at the very best an inappropriate remark.

"Maybe, singed is too strong a term." Darcy replied. Elizabeth looked back at him but could read nothing in his face. She took a chance and looked in his eyes, his dark gaze capturing hers with words unspoken. Her cheeks pinked, and she looked away back at the safer environs of Colonel Fitzwilliam. Butterflies fluttered in her stomach. *Now what brought that on?*

CHAPTER 2

"My nephew always makes dining that much more lively." Lady Catherine de Bourgh waved her handkerchief at the two men seated at her table. She was making a point to the guests in attendance: Mr. and Mrs. Collins and Elizabeth Bennet. "My daughter, Anne, is always so excited to see Mr. Darcy, aren't you my dear?" She inclined her head at a pale young woman sitting next to her at the table. Anne gave a half-hearted smile in return.

"Yes, I always look forward to seeing my relations who bring news of other places." It was the most she had said all evening, and with that statement, she seemed out of breath.

"Are you well, dear?" Lady Catherine asked. "Perhaps, this is too much for you?"

Anne sat up straighter smiling, but even with her will, she seemed small. "I am quite fine," she replied. "The air is dryer than I like this evening, but I can measure up." The pale yellow gown she was wearing did little to add to her look; in fact, it lent a sallow color to her already wan countenance. Her hair was carefully done with curls and small gems that added a glitter to her look, but nothing could erase the dark circles under her eyes and dull skin.

"When the time is right and the person amenable, then a match can be made." Lady Catherine looked at Mr. Darcy when she spoke, but he ignored her.

"The ladies enjoy walking; we came upon them earlier today in the woods between Mrs. Collins' home and here," Colonel Fitzwilliam changed the subject, before Mr. Darcy could respond. Not that it appeared Mr. Darcy planned on making any response, Elizabeth noted. This seemed to be an old bone of contention.

They passed the evening pleasantly enough, with Lady Catherine insisting that Elizabeth play the pianoforte, much to the delight of everyone there and the disguised chagrin of herself. She played and smiled, but refused to sing. One could only be pushed so far. Elizabeth received applause for her efforts. She noticed Mr. Darcy and Colonel Fitzwilliam looking on appreciatively and wondered which of the gentlemen's interest she liked the most.

Mr. Darcy, dark, distant and aloof, held a certain attraction for her, although Colonel Fitzwilliam was an open book, full of jest and compliments. Elizabeth liked puzzles, and Mr. Darcy was certainly an intriguing enigma.

She wondered why Lady Catherine kept foisting – and there was no other word for it – her daughter on Mr. Darcy. The Lady's hints were less than subtle. Elizabeth also wondered why Mr. Darcy did not object outright, just looked uncomfortable enough to be amusing. Clearly, Mr. Darcy was not interested in marrying Anne out of amicability, and there seemed no spark from her side either.

Anne did not regard Mr. Darcy as one would a cad, but she seemed to light up in conversation with Colonel Fitzwilliam. As did Miss Lucas, though the young woman was far too intimidated to say more than a few mumbled words before allowing the conversation to continue on without her. To Mr. Darcy, Anne gave a bored look, one of forbearance for her mother's wishes and nothing more.

And for Mr. Darcy's part, he gave perfunctory conversation snippets raised out of courtesy more than anything else. He seemed less interested in Anne than the potted ficus plant that sat near the door, and it needed watering.

Elizabeth caught him looking at her. When she returned to her seat from the pianoforte, he stood to help her with her chair, although she needed no such help.

"Thank you, Mr. Darcy," she smiled at him.

He bowed curtly and resumed his seat.

Elizabeth had the impression her earning Mr. Darcy's solicitude was not to Lady Catherine's liking, because the Lady regarded the exchange with a sour look, down-turned mouth forming a thin line, eyes squinting as if facing direct sunlight.

Lady Catherine was in a well-lit, but not overly so, drawing room. There was no reason to squint, Elizabeth noted to herself, unless one were attempting to frown and failing that, settling for a squint and a sniff.

She is displeased at Mr. Darcy's kindness toward me. That amused Elizabeth, causing her to smile at

Lady Catherine and earn herself another squinty sniff.

Colonel Fitzwilliam and Anne were engaged in a conversation that was interrupted by Lady Catherine. "You should talk with Mr. Darcy, Anne."

"About what, Mother?" Anne asked, her gaze traveling from Mr. Darcy to Lady Catherine.

"Well, about your plans for the future," Lady Catherine said. "Surely, you have some ideas for when we go to Town, something that would interest a man of his stature and means." Silence followed her statement.

Mr. Collins stepped into the hush, waxing poetic about life in the Ton. "It is a time when all things are alight in London, where you can dance the night away at balls and private parties; is it not, Lady Catherine? I mean, everyone who is anyone is there, and the fashion…" he breathed in as if he could smell high society, "it is without equal I'm told."

"You have attended balls in Town?" Mr. Darcy asked, and Elizabeth saw it again – that slight upturn in his lips, and the twinkle in his dark eyes. He was joking with Mr. Collins.

"Me, no! I am a man of the cloth. However, I

have heard tales and stories related to me. It sounds wonderful."

"I should like to attend balls in Town," Miss Lucas said softly. Her gaze drifted to Col. Fitzwilliam who in turn watched Miss de Bourgh.

"I find balls tiresome," Mr. Darcy replied, dismissing Mr. Collins with a slight wave of his hand.

"Unless, you are with the right person," Lady Catherine put in. The words 'like my daughter, Anne….' hung in the air unspoken.

"That is true, Aunt," Darcy agreed, but his gaze did not go to her daughter, but to Elizabeth, who returned his look with one of mild curiosity. His lip quirked, and she felt a flutter in her stomach in response. Mr. Darcy was quite a curious creature, a mystery to solve. Elizabeth wasn't sure if she liked or loathed his subtle humor. Mr. Collins did not see where Darcy was having him on. And, Darcy let him put his foot in his proverbial mouth more than once that evening.

Elizabeth found it both funny and annoying. No one less endowed with intelligence should be laughed at, but it was her cousin, which made that inference less offending. He was such an obsequious person, and she laughed at him. Even his wife found humor in his long soliloquys to Lady Catherine.

If he could fall to his knees – no, lay flat out on his paunchy stomach to let Lady Catherine walk over him and not muddy her shoes – he would do so with pleasure and thank her for the privilege. So, Darcy's bit of humor at Mr. Collins' expense was funny. Elizabeth realized it was only her guilt as his guest, and more importantly, best friend to his wife, that gave Elizabeth pause.

Colonel Fitzwilliam resumed his conversation with Anne, and they spent the rest of the evening laughing and what Elizabeth determined was subtly flirting with each other. In her last visit to the de Bourgh estate, Anne seemed almost disinterested in life, but with the Colonel, she was livelier, engaged, her cheeks reddened and her eyes had a twinkle.

This had a disturbing effect on her mother, because although Lady Catherine loved both her nephews, Colonel Fitzwilliam had only his military stipend to live on and provide for a family. Mr. Darcy was a far better prospect in her opinion. However, love knows or cares little of status or wealth, and this instance was no exception.

You are much like my mother, Elizabeth thought. It was not a bad thing that a mother would want what was best for her daughter. Lady Catherine, like her own mother, could be aggressive to a fault in trying to secure it. Both Mr. Darcy and Anne were little inclined to oblige.

"How long will you be with us?" Mr. Darcy's voice interrupted Elizabeth's musings. She blushed with the idea that he had caught her wool gathering and smiled.

"At least another fortnight, maybe more," she answered. "Then I will return home, I believe. I also might take in London and visit with my aunt and uncle. My aunt asked for me to come and visit, as I have not been there in quite a while." Elizabeth kept her gaze to the left of his, finishing her sentence and looking at him directly at last.

If it was possible, Elizabeth realized that his dark gaze darkened, and she realized, with some consternation, that she felt like she could fall into those obsidian pools. There was something about the way he looked at her that made her stomach clinch.

It wasn't until after Elizabeth looked away that she realized she had been holding her breath. Carefully and silently, she exhaled lest he know the effect he was having on her.

It happened a couple more times over the

course of the evening, and each time her heart quickened. The feeling was both nerve-wracking and wonderful, the latter a betrayal of her firm determination not to get wrapped up and lose her objectivity. That appeared to be a losing battle as Elizabeth's feelings took charge. She was enamored. But love differed from interest or passion. Elizabeth knew this. She had always depended on her mind in all things: rational judgment, keen observation and quiet objectivity to form an opinion of someone.

In this instance, her mind seemed to be betraying her.

Yes, Mr. Darcy was an attractive man, even when he was being severe and reserved, but she kept seeing cracks in that detached armor which belied the image he had carefully constructed and portrayed. Behind that armor was a mystery, a nice mystery she guessed the slight quirk of his lips betrayed.

Mr. Darcy had a sense of humor, and in conversation, he withheld much of his own thoughts when dealing with buffoonery like her cousin exhibited. However, in a single joke, delivered with the seriousness of an undertaker, she gleaned some of how his mind worked. Or, at least she thought she did.

Was she just making all of this up, based on a flight of fancy? Infatuation?

Could she really know all this from the lifting of an eyebrow, the quirking of his very kissable lips?

Stop that, she admonished herself. *You cannot be thinking of kissing the man. You barely know him. The heart wants what the heart wants.*

Elizabeth looked at a vase of flowers near the window, regrouping. Her thoughts gave her pause, and her silence apparently caused him some concern, because he gave her a shy smile when his aunt was engaged in conversation with Colonel Fitzwilliam. It was fleeting, but it reached his eyes which twinkled in response, and she felt hot with the attention.

Her previous opinion of him evaporated. There was a lot more to Mr. Darcy that she wanted to know; she needed to know for her own sanity. If he could bring forth such feelings in her in the parlor while his aunt played matchmaker, what other capabilities did he possess? Clearly, he was not interested in Anne which was just as well. She seemed enamored of the colonel, and he was reciprocating, much to Miss Lucas' visible dismay.

She is much like my mother when it comes to getting her daughter married, although if I told the great Lady Catherine that, she would have my head for such a rude and 'wholly untrue' reflection.

What Lady Catherine hoped was if Anne was left without conversation, she would naturally gravitate towards Mr. Darcy. What happened was the opposite, and judging from the sharpness of her tone, this vexed her. Anne sat as close as was proper to Colonel Fitzwilliam. She ignored Mr. Darcy, leaving him to shower Elizabeth with veiled considerations. He was not flirting, per se. He was more open, showing her what lay behind the wall of propriety and detachment he maintained.

Why in the world was her mind spiraling out of control like this? It was just a smile, but then he gave her another smile, secret from everyone else, just for her. Because she was facing the group, she felt it indecent to smile back at him. So, carefully, lest someone notice, she inclined her head, quirking her lips as he did. She stared into his eyes for a moment, then looking away at some perceived mote of dust or shadow on the back of Lady Catherine's chair.

When their eyes met again, his lip quirked and the softness of his look spoke volumes.

They had reached some understanding and nary a word spoken. Few gentlemen in Elizabeth's experience could do that. Maybe, because she and he were in harmony; their rapport seemed complete.

With that realization, Elizabeth felt the pull of him. She wondered what would happen next, but only for a moment. Best not dwell upon that over which she had no control.

CHAPTER 3

B ook in hand, Elizabeth headed to her favorite reading nook, a small tree at the top of a hill, fifteen minutes or so from Charlotte's house. Maria did not wake before eleven in the morning unless prodded, and Charlotte had insisted Elizabeth feel comfortable walking about wherever she wished in the morning, with or without her friend who preferred less active morning pursuits. While it impressed Elizabeth how well Charlotte managed Mr. Collins, she could not imagine such a life for herself. Elizabeth wished to marry for love.

Mr. Darcy's secret smile hung in Elizabeth's memory, making her skin heat and her stomach flutter.

It was no longer their only secret.

Infatuation is not love, she reminded herself. Mr. and Mrs. Bennet had married for infatuation, and they barely tolerated each other. Elizabeth would not allow herself the same weakness.

At the same time, infatuation could be seen as a root for love. It was all too complicated, and Elizabeth tried to push this confusion from her mind. The day was fair, and she had hours to read. Or converse, if a certain someone happened upon her.

Elizabeth's cheeks heated.

Having reached the top of the hill, Elizabeth unrolled the small blanket that she'd been carrying, placed it in the nook of the tree, and sat down carefully so as not to dirty her frock any more than the bottom fringes had gotten mucking through the muddier patches of the meadows. The last thing she wanted was to walk home with a damp and dirty posterior, but the blanket would help her avoid such embarrassing circumstances.

Elizabeth hoped Mr. Darcy found her this morning, as he had done nearly every morning since their dinner at Lady Catherine's.

Mr. Darcy would ride up on one of his magnificent steeds, bowing when he came upon her as though by happenstance. Except happenstance could not be such a regular occurrence.

Upon finding her, unchaperoned, though neither acknowledged this impropriety, he would bow, climb down and ask her to walk with him.

After an hour of reading, Elizabeth heard hoof-beats, and, truthfully irked he had taken so long, hatched an idea for some fun. Instead of waiting for him by the tree, where he had surely seen her, she waited for the familiar shape of his horse to be hidden by the foliage and, leaving book and blanket at the tree's base, swung up onto the branches and hid.

Hide and Go Seek. Would he seek her?

Elizabeth hoped.

Mr. Darcy walked around the base of the tree and even called out. "Excuse me? Miss?"

He did not say her name. Though she could only see the top of his head, she imagined his frown, a task made more difficult by their days of pleasant acquaintanceship.

Mr. Darcy started to walk back towards his horse. He muttered something under his breath, his hands fisted.

Could a simple game so easily frustrate him?

Perhaps. She hardly knew him, infatuation aside.

Elizabeth, light as a feather, dropped to the ground.

"Mr. Darcy!" she called out.

Mr. Darcy turned, his mouth an "O" of astonishment.

"Miss Elizabeth! Where were you?" he demanded.

"You were looking for me?" Elizabeth grinned.

"What if someone had abducted you? There are brigands in this part."

"So close to your aunt's estate? Mr. Darcy, you are overwrought."

"A servant woman was abducted from a neighboring town. Richard spoke with their constable. And there have been thefts. Jewels. Gold."

"Of which I have none." Was this why Mr. Darcy had been meeting her 'by chance'? Concern she might be seized by brigands? Elizabeth was uncertain if she was flattered or annoyed. If he feared for her safety, why had he told her nothing of the danger?

"I was right here." Elizabeth glanced upwards.

"In a tree?" His scowl deepened. "You will not play such games again."

How little he knew her to demand such a thing. And to think, she had begun to imagine a future with him. Now, he treated her like a fool. Or a child.

Elizabeth said, "I had no intention to disturb your morning ride. I am well and enjoying a lovely book."

"I—" Mr. Darcy scratched his cheek. "It is no interruption. Quite a fair morning, is it not?"

Elizabeth nodded. Once they had finished discussing the weather, they might move onto Lady Catherine's table settings and other riveting topics. And yet, Elizabeth's flash of anger cooled at his obvious discomfiture. He cared for her welfare. He might be zealous in his pursuit of it, but she appreciated his interest.

They walked to the tree and sat. Mr. Darcy asked, "What are you reading?"

"You will think me silly, if I tell you," she began, a blush gracing her cheeks.

"You? Silly? Never." He reached for the book and she withdrew her hand. "It's a fairy tale of sorts about a water spirit named Undine. My father got it for Kitty, but she wasn't interested. I found it to be tolerable."

He reached over relieving her of the book.

"Undine by Friedrich de la Motte Fouqué," he read aloud. "Undine is a water creature?"

"Yes." she retrieved the book, turning it face down in her lap.

"I had not imagined you liking fairy tales."

"Well, it is well written," she replied as if that was a defense. "The theme is interesting." She did not understand why she felt discomfited.

"I'm sure it is. I could not see you reading it if it were not."

You are handsome, Mr. Darcy, Elizabeth thought, *in so many ways. My attraction for you grows, because I have caught glimpses of that wonderful person you keep hidden.* Elizabeth shook her head looking away from him feeling the heat in her cheeks and other places she would rather not ponder. *Now, what brought that on?*

"Are you well, Miss Elizabeth?" She felt him, his voice deep, soft spoken, and when she looked back at him, his gaze was all curiosity with a slight smile gracing his lips. "You seem to be a bit flushed.

"No, I was just thinking about something," she replied. *If only you knew how much my affections rise just gazing upon your form. I wonder if this is lust, love or simple friendship.* She had little experience except in friendship, and never a male friend except for that cad Wickham whose friendship was false.

Be careful what you wish for, Elizabeth. She had wished for high passion, a love affair that would last for all time with a man who swept her up and took her to a magical place. Mr. Darcy was looking like that man in her dreams. And, oh the dreams she was having... *No, this is not merely friendship.*

"Would it be impolite if I asked you about what?" How long had she been sitting there ruminating?

"Flower arrangements," Elizabeth sprang to her feet, nearly running into him. She put out a hand out and stopped herself, and touched his chest, taking a moment too long to feel it. He didn't seem to mind, his smile widening, and if she was not mistaken, she thought she saw his gaze darken. "I plan on doing some flower arranging with Charlotte this afternoon." She righted herself, withdrawing her hand reluctantly.

"Flower arranging," he let out a full-throated laugh. "That must be an intense affair considering your look."

"It can be," she replied. His words were not lost on her; he was teasing her. "I also plan on doing some knitting, and maybe some needlepoint."

Mr. Darcy threw up his hands placating her and stepping back. "That is wonderful! I meant nothing by my earlier remarks, Miss Elizabeth, nothing at all. I know little of the concentration it takes for those sorts of ladies' activities."

He was still smiling, now standing and for a little while, she just basked in being so close to him. He smelled of leather and soap, and Elizabeth breathed in. With each deep breath, she could imagine him kissing her, passionately, wantonly and with pure abandon.

She imagined him taking her in his arms, kissing her, at first hesitant and then with more fervor. Elizabeth met his gaze. His pupils widened, and his gaze pinned her. He wanted her, and she wanted him, and if he kissed her, it would sweep them both away. Propriety thrown to the winds, she reached up and gently caressed his cheek. When her hand touched Mr. Darcy, he trembled, closing his eyes, a slight smile gracing his lips.

"Elizabeth," he whispered. "You bewitch me." Mr. Darcy's voice was soft, husky.

"We must stop," Elizabeth withdrew her hand from him, and he opened his eyes, looking at her.

Infatuation was not love. She had to be certain something deeper lived beneath this passion, lest she make a terrible mistake.

If Elizabeth kept gazing at him, it could lead to something neither of them were ready for. She stepped away from him, took a breath, regaining her comportment as she walked. He dutifully followed, until she slowed down again. "I am returning to the parsonage to help Charlotte with breakfast."

The sun was still low in the sky, and while Elizabeth wanted to stay in Mr. Darcy's company, she thought better of it. She had twisted the rules of propriety enough without ruining her good name. And she never would want Mr. Darcy to marry her under coercion. Elizabeth wanted his offer out of love, an intense feeling of deep affection and nothing less.

"May I attend you to your gate," Mr. Darcy bowed slightly as he spoke, the serious, formal side of him coming to the fore. Was this the same man who had laughed and teased her earlier? *You are a complicated man, Mr. Darcy.*

"Yes, if that is convenient."

"It is my pleasure." He stopped her and handed her a small flower, white with a bit of green on the stalk. He also had an identical flower in his hand. "Pray, I hope you do not consider this too forward, but would you condescend to take this small flower to press in your book, a remembrance of our time together this morning. I will keep this second flower in my vest pocket close to my heart.

Darcy knew that it was at the lengths of propriety and probably over the line, but he wanted her to remember him when they were apart. He did it on a whim, but now in the light of reality, his heart hitched at the deeper meaning it held. Would Elizabeth accept it from him? If she did, it would mean the world to him, that she accepted him on a deeper level than shallow conversation. Darcy was rewarded with a smile and a sparkle of wonderment in her gaze at him.

"That is so thoughtful, Mr. Darcy." If Elizabeth accepted it, this meant a deepening of their relationship, and although she would not allow herself to succumb to meaningless passion, she was developing deeper feelings for Mr. Darcy.

Propriety dictated Elizabeth reject his offering, but she was far beyond the bounds of propriety already. Elizabeth took the flower and placed it on one of the inside pages. With the acceptance, her cheeks heated. He would keep an identical flower with him. This was a secret commitment, something stronger than the kiss she wished she had allowed herself, and she relished their connection.

Perhaps infatuation could lead to something more.

CHAPTER 4

I must be in love.

When I look into Miss Elizabeth's dark eyes, I am captured. In her gaze, I see my heart, and I am swept away. Miss Elizabeth is the balm that assuages my loneliness. When we are together, I am at peace, and we are one.

But how do I tell her? And when?

From the Personal Journal of Mr. Fitzwilliam Darcy

FITZWILLIAM DARCY SAT IN THE LIBRARY, A CUP of lukewarm coffee on a small table beside him. He was tired, and it was only mid-morning. Unofficial courting could do that, and he had his hands full with Miss Elizabeth Bennet.

Ignoring his need to kiss her, to love her completely and with great passion, took its toll. He reminded himself he did this to protect her. Elizabeth was not one to heed warnings of brigands or abduction. She had told him as much the first and only time he had attempted to broach the subject.

As to the rest...

Though he admired Miss Elizabeth Bennet, and she did not act as a social climber, he had to be certain of her affection. Too many ladies' interests stemmed from his inheritance and lands.

Including his aunt's ambitions for Anne.

Darcy rubbed his palm over his forehead. He wished Bingley were here. Not that Bingley had any sense when judging women.

No, better Bingley was absent.

"Darcy, there you are." Richard Fitzwilliam strode into the library. "We have a problem."

"The brigands?"

"I believe the issue is more than simple brigands."

Darcy yawned. "I apologize." He sipped his coffee. "You said ladies were being accosted, their jewels stolen."

"Yes, and a servant was abducted, which is the crux of the problem. Miss Emily Davis was not seized from a carriage! According to those the constable and I questioned, she was going by foot to meet with a local fruit seller who often allowed her to ride on his wagon with the vegetables when she visited her mother on her half-days.

"Perhaps the fruit seller was involved?"

"Doubtful. He waited until dusk for her arrival, and others in the villagers confirmed it, before returning to his home. And the fruit seller showed genuine distress at Miss Davis' disappearance. Worse, she is not the only servant gone missing these past few months."

"Servants run away."

"Attractive young maids, many of whom are rumored to be overly close with their male employers?" Richard sighed. "Something in this sits ill."

Darcy nodded. Likely the young maids were given a sum and sent off to raise their bastards before the evidence of the gentleman's infidelity became obvious. While such behavior disgusted Darcy, it was not uncommon in his class. Darcy, having seen the consequence of his father's failure on his family, vowed never to allow himself such a weakness.

If the missing women were servants, then likely they had run off, not abducted, and Elizabeth was safe. Thus Darcy no longer had an excuse to keep happening upon her during her morning walks.

"There is something more sinister afoot," Richard declared. "We must speak with and warn Lady Catherine's servants and those of the village."

"Are you certain this is necessary?" Darcy asked.

"I am certain of nothing. But my gut tells me something is wrong. And that instinct has kept me alive thus far. You will need to speak with Aunt Catherine. If I ask, she may ignore me, but she denies you nothing."

"I will." Darcy did not doubt his cousin's instincts. When they were children, he had snatched Darcy back from crossing the log over the stream, as they had done countless times throughout that summer.

A minute later, after they had climbed down to the bank to determine how to cross, that branch had broken. Darcy would have broken a leg or his neck, if he had crossed that day.

Richard clapped a hand on Darcy's shoulder. "Good. And I will warn the Collinses and their guests, Miss Lucas and Miss Bennet."

Darcy's expression froze at the mention of Elizabeth's name. It was only a moment, but Richard's eyes narrowed. "I see."

"There is nothing for you to see."

"It is not Miss Lucas, I presume."

"No!"

Richard smiled. "Aunt Catherine will be appalled."

Darcy shrugged. Aunt Catherine was often appalled.

CHAPTER 5

Elizabeth Bennet was grateful for the expansive lands of Lady Catherine de Bourgh, even if she wasn't that fond of the lady herself.

Mr. Darcy had declared, "You will not play such games again."

And so she had played such games. Not hiding for long enough to cause him true concern. Just enough to have him look. Perhaps call out her name.

Darcy came down the path, dismounting at her borrowed blanket, a book of folklore left open atop it. He looked around. Elizabeth hid behind a tall tree, holding her breath and standing as still as she could.

Elizabeth's infatuation grew. She had pushed him away, but she wanted that kiss. Just as she hid, hoping he would search, she waited, hoping he would try again, press his lips to hers and...

Elizabeth heard him walk up to the tree and stop. It would give the game away if she stepped out into view so close, so she sank further into a cut in the tree's side. One snap of a twig and the jig would be up, but there was no crack or snap, and she waited.

There was a rustling on the side of the English oak and then, to her surprise, his footsteps receded. A minute later, hoofbeats. As the sound diminished, she stepped out from the tree and walked to her blanket. A red rose caught her attention at the base of the oak and beneath it was a second book.

"Grimm's Fairy Tales," she read the book title aloud. Elizabeth smelled the rose — sweet and fresh — how kind. She started reading the introduction. A twig snapped behind her, and she looked up startled.

"Good morning," Mr. Darcy said, eyes twinkling.

"You came back?" Elizabeth dropped the book, stood, and curtsied.

"I will always come back." Mr. Darcy bowed. "Shall we read?"

Reading, so close and still atop the small blanket seemed somehow more scandalous than a stroll. Which was nonsense, but Elizabeth said, "A walk? If it pleases you."

"It does." Mr. Darcy offered his arm.

She took it, and he rested a gloved hand atop hers. As they walked, he brushed his fingers over her forearm. Their hips brushed. His scent, sandalwood, sweat, and something else, washed over her.

Having him so close made her stomach tighten. *What would it be like to kiss him? Will he be tender or intense and forceful?* She hoped for a little of both.

Elizabeth should have been nervous, walking unchaperoned with a man who had given her not a declaration but only a flower, now flat and dry between the pages of a book. Yet she could not doubt his feelings nor, if she were honest, her own.

"I thought you might like another book I found entertaining," Mr. Darcy said.

Elizabeth looked at him, noting the slight smile on his lips. He had upended the game with this action, and she felt a blush rising on her cheeks. "Why, thank you, Mr. Darcy," she managed. "I will hope I enjoy it as much as you did. I was not aware that you liked fairy tales."

He touched her elbow leading her back on to the path. "It is not my first choice for reading, but I was curious, after seeing your Undine novel, what you found so attractive. Grimm's book is a bit heartier, more adventurous, and darker than Undine."

"You read Undine?" Elizabeth's eyebrows rose.

"As I said." Darcy bit back a chuckle, feigning a look of complete innocence. "I am glad I came upon you. I look forward to our talks, and would have missed giving you the book."

"And, the rose," Elizabeth dared. "It was a lovely thought."

Mr. Darcy smiled.

"But your horse?" Had he sent his steed on alone? Abandoned horses often returned to their stables. That seemed quite a risk for a mount so fine.

"Tied beside a field, feasting on grasses," he replied. "His name is Whisper. I do not believe you have been formally introduced."

Elizabeth smiled. "Informally, for certain, we are acquainted, but formally, not yet."

"Allow me." Mr. Darcy led her towards his

horse. When he picked up the horse's tether, it nuzzled him, and he responded with part of an apple retrieved from his coat pocket.

Elizabeth pulled her glove free, and Mr. Darcy's gaze lingered on her bare hand. She held it out. He took it and he placed an apple slice in it for her to feed to Whisper. His fingers lingered a moment on her naked hand, and her breath hitched as if the heat of it scorched her. His touch was gentle and all too brief.

Elizabeth fed the horse, aware of his proximity. It was closer than propriety demanded, and she never wanted it to end.

Elizabeth felt warm in his presence. She longed for him to touch her again, as the world with all of its complications faded with the brush of his fingers

"Shall we return to your tree?"

The spell was broken, and Elizabeth was irritated at its passing.

"No."

"Did you want to do something else?" Again, she saw that slight smirk gracing his lips, and his gaze darkened. He wanted her; of this she was sure. And, she wanted him, more and more with each meeting. The game could not dampen the feelings that swelled in her bosom and tightening of her stomach she had felt with no other gentleman.

The words caught in her throat, and she could not breathe.

I wish you would kiss me.

"May I?" Mr. Darcy stepped closer.

Elizabeth nodded.

Mr. Darcy kissed her, at first chaste and hesitant, then more boldly as her lips softened at his touch. Elizabeth was not prepared for this cascade of feelings. Her body felt afire. She had pushed him away once before, for propriety's sake, but the dam was broken, and Elizabeth didn't want to stop. She stood on her tiptoes, hands on his shoulders for balance.

More please, her body begged.

Mr. Darcy released her from the kiss, and she took in a breath. Her heart was racing, and her knees felt weak. "My word," was all she managed.

He was so much taller than she, and the strength rippling through him took her breath away.

"I can do it again," Darcy offered, smiling like the cat that ate the canary. "Or, we can walk."

Elizabeth whispered. "All we do is walk."

Darcy chuckled, "I thought you enjoyed walking." There it was again, that oh-so-innocent Darcy, teasing and playful.

Is that smile reserved only for me? "I like to do other things, you know," she snapped back at him.

"Yes, reading," Mr. Darcy said, his expression grave.

Elizabeth smacked his shoulder. "And *other* things."

"I see."

Mr. Darcy kissed her again. Her lips, robbing her of breath. He kissed her cheek, her jaw, and neck. Her pulse hammered.

It was too much. Too wonderful. She wanted more, and that frightened her. She stiffened.

"Miss Elizabeth?" His breath tickled her skin.

Elizabeth had vowed to marry for love, but how could she know this was love? Her parents had succumbed to lust, and now they lived separate lives within the same house. Mr. Bennet mocked his wife and Mrs. Bennet pretended his jests proved his affection.

"I will not hurt you," Mr. Darcy said.

Perhaps she would hurt him. Or they would hurt each other? Elizabeth feared Lydia's excessive flirting a danger to her virtue, and now, Elizabeth was the wanton.

A gasp. "Eliza!"

And worse.

"Miss Elizabeth Bennet! Oh my *Goodness!*"

Elizabeth's guts turned to ice. She jumped from Mr. Darcy's embrace.

The voice belonged to Mr. William Collins, and Elizabeth was ruined.

CHAPTER 6

Elizabeth and Mr. Darcy?

Charlotte did not know what to make of it. Maria stood beside Charlotte, her mouth parted in shock. "What are you doing?" she asked, as if it was not perfectly obvious.

What had Elizabeth been thinking to engage in a dalliance with Mr. Darcy of all people, the nephew of their patroness? Elizabeth did not engage in dalliances at all, as far as Charlotte understood. Elizabeth had told Charlotte about the stolen kiss at the Assembly when she was sixteen. She had told Charlotte of her brief interest in Mr. Wickham, and her disgust when he turned his attention elsewhere upon realizing Elizabeth's dowry was small.

But Elizabeth had mentioned nothing of *this*. Charlotte wondered if she knew her friend at all.

Charlotte could not save Elizabeth from the consequences of their discovering her and Mr. Darcy. If Mr. Darcy did not propose, Elizabeth was ruined. Even with a proposal and hasty marriage, Elizabeth's reputation was tarnished. This was a disaster.

Charlotte blamed herself. If she had come upon them alone, they might keep it quiet. But her husband could not be trusted to keep secrets, not one such as this.

To Elizabeth, this was a nightmare come true. She and Mr. Darcy had not discussed marriage. What if he assumed she had set him up for a compromise? He was a man of honor, and he would offer for her.

What if he did not?

What if he did?

Elizabeth's stomach churned.

"William," Charlotte began. "This might not be as it appears." Though it had appeared, in Charlotte's mind, delicious. She hated the jealousy she felt for her friend's obvious passion. Though she was satisfied, mostly, in her life as Mrs. William Collins, his attentions were more something to be endured than relished. At least, when they kissed, he was silent.

"Charlotte, you saw the pair of them. He... umm... her neck—" Mr. Collins looked at the ground. "This will not do. And Miss Bennet, a guest in my parsonage. Mr. Darcy, you must make this right. And, Miss Bennet, for shame! You're not a young, naive girl. You ought to know better."

"I have made an offer," Darcy replied quickly. "You interrupted us, but now you are the first to know that we are engaged."

That brought Mr. Collins up short. "You have?"

"Certainly."

"But Miss Anne de Bourgh!"

"Miss Anne and I have made no promises to each other."

"How romantic!" Miss Lucas exclaimed, clapping her hands together.

Tears filled Elizabeth's eyes. Darcy had just lied. He had made no mention of marriage before. And now, here they were in the worst of compromising positions. She had vowed to marry for love or deep affection at the very least. Now, with this, how could she be sure of anything?

They had lust for each other, but what about love? Would there ever be a deep affection that allowed each of them the comfort of being friends and lovers? Elizabeth wasn't sure the answers to any of these questions, because their courtship was now over, both he and she conscripted into being Mr. and Mrs. Darcy.

Mr. Collins eyes widened. "Then, as Miss Elizabeth is my cousin, you and I shall be family."

"I suppose." Mr. Darcy did not sound pleased, nor did Elizabeth blame him.

"And also the Lady Catherine de Bourgh—!" Mr. Collins whistled a breath through his teeth. "A tremendous honor. Just tremendous! Charlotte, did you hear?"

"William, let us not overwhelm the happy couple with our felicitations."

Tears rolled down Elizabeth's cheeks. Charlotte handed Elizabeth her handkerchief and put her arm around her.

"Yes. Certainly. Miss Elizabeth seems overwrought." Mr. Collins patted her hand. "There, there, Elizabeth," he cleared his throat. "An offer was made. Mr. Darcy is doing the honorable thing, and your reputation is intact. I assume your chaperone is nearby, or did you come upon each other by happenstance?

"Happenstance, but I felt the time was perfect for my proposal."

"Yes. Perfect." Mr. Collins patted Elizabeth's hand again. Her fingers clenched.

Elizabeth should object to this proposal. But if she did, she destroyed not only her own reputation, but also the futures of her sisters.

"Do excuse us, Mr. Darcy," Charlotte interjected, trying to stop her husband's chatter.

Mr. Collins took a breath and then continued, "You can see what it looked like. Without the proper context, one can make all manner of presumptions. Lady Catherine must be informed, and while Miss Anne de Bourgh's heart may be broken, in matters of the heart, there can be no telling outcomes."

"William, dear, Elizabeth must return with us to the parsonage."

"Yes. We would not want another to see you and gain a wrongful impression. Maria, do not speak of what you have seen. And do not believe this is a proper way to conduct a courtship. Though Mr. Darcy's intentions were honorable, one cannot count on such from any young gentleman."

Maria glanced back at Elizabeth and Mr. Darcy. Her eyes were wide and she gave Elizabeth a quick smile. Elizabeth forced herself to smile back. The expression did little to mask the terror in her heart.

Mrs. Elizabeth Darcy. She had no choice now.

"I shall inform Lady Catherine of the situation," Mr. Collins added. "And your intentions to do honorably by my cousin."

Mr. Darcy paled. "That is not necessary. I will tell her myself!"

"It is no bother, Mr. Darcy," Collins puffed. "This is wonderful news, cousin!" He grinned at Mr. Darcy.

"I will tell my aunt the news myself," Darcy said again. "I insist."

"Yes, she must be told! Immediately!" Mr. Collins waved at Mr. Darcy, smiling as he followed Miss Lucas, Elizabeth and his wife back up the path.

CHAPTER 7

Lady Catherine de Bourgh paced the length of her library, clasping Mr. Collins' all too delighted missive of two full pages. She was not gauche enough to reduce herself to foul language, instead detailing Miss Elizabeth Bennet's lowly status – the daughter of a baronet with her family estate entailed – and the clear faults in her character, which the young lady made no efforts to correct.

The nerve of that chit, believing she could manipulate Fitzwilliam's urges to bring forth a proposal of marriage.

The gall!

Despite Lady Catherine's urging Fitzwilliam to take time to consider Miss Bennet's character and their situation, Fitzwilliam had taken off for Town to secure a special license, insisting he and Miss Bennet would be married as soon as possible.

Shameful. The entire business. And wholly unacceptable.

"What to do?" she asked herself, her voice punctuated by the rapid tread of her footsteps. Up. Back.

All was not lost. Fitzwilliam was doing the honorable thing, but if Lady Catherine could persuade Miss Bennet to leave before he returned, then she might salvage her daughter's future.

An offering of funds would suffice. The Bennets were near as poor as church mice, and Lady Catherine had funds to send them on their way.

Except, Fitzwilliam would follow Miss Bennet back to her home, if only to be certain she rejected his proposal in truth.

If he did, his heart would break. Better that than to be saddled to an unsuitable wife.

But what if Miss Bennet did not accept Lady Catherine's generous offer? Miss Bennet was no fool, for all she lacked in refinement. What offered funds could measure to becoming the mistress of Pemberley?

Lady Catherine sighed.

Sat.

There was another solution. Lord Braithwaite was visiting in the neighboring village, and he was known to solve problems of this sort.

Lady Catherine rang for a servant who brought her writing desk. It was early afternoon. If Lady Catherine wrote quickly, by the Lord's grace, there would be time enough to make arrangements before Fitzwilliam returned.

Lady Catherine was no monster. She would offer a payment first. After that, she washed her hands of the whole sick affair.

For Anne's sake.

It was a mother's duty to ensure her daughter's happiness.

CHAPTER 8

The next afternoon, Charlotte barged into Elizabeth's guest room and insisted she rise for tea.

"Even Maria is awake and out with her paints, Lizzy. Come, it is a lovely day. You must be hungry."

"You have heard nothing from Mr. Darcy?" Elizabeth said.

"Not yet. But one of the village ladies saw his carriage depart yesterday afternoon. He is likely to London to get a Special License."

"He would need an audience with the Archbishop of Canterbury." And while Mr. Darcy's uncle was an Earl, as Lady Catherine had opined on at length, Mr. Darcy himself was not a peer. Would he even receive such an audience? Let alone the expense of the license. Perhaps he had fled to London, not to return. Elizabeth was not sure what to wish. If Mr. Collins had kept his mouth shut and Mr. Darcy fled, Charlotte would speak nothing of Elizabeth's compromise, and Elizabeth could go on as before.

Except Elizabeth missed Mr. Darcy. She did not wish to coerce him into marriage, but she had hoped they might have a future together.

"I suppose Mr. Collins has told everyone in the village of my... situation?"

"Lady Catherine wrote and somehow compelled him to silence. In truth, the position we found the pair of you in... my husband would prefer not to seem a party to... you understand."

"Mr. Collins will keep his silence then?"

Charlotte shrugged. "As well as expected. He drops hints. Fortunately, they are obscure."

"Perhaps this can be fixed."

"Fixed? You do not wish to marry him?"

Elizabeth sighed. "I do not know!" She clutched the duvet. She had cried the pillow damp the night before. Now, tears threatened again. She took a breath, trying to recapture the joy of that morning with Mr. Darcy before everything had gone wrong.

"Come, have tea. You must also be hungry."

Elizabeth wished to say she was not, but her stomach growled.

Charlotte laughed. "I will meet you in the drawing room."

Twenty-minutes later, Elizabeth reluctantly walked into the drawing room and sat.

To her dismay, Mr. Collins was with his wife. He whispered something to her. When Elizabeth was announced, Mr. Collins looked up, stood, and greeted her. "Miss Elizabeth. Cousin. Sit." He waved towards the empty chair, thankfully at Charlotte's other side.

Elizabeth sat. A maid poured the tea which Elizabeth received gratefully. It gave her extra moments to collect her thoughts. Charlotte's sympathetic mien told Elizabeth that she understood more than her husband did. Elizabeth wished for Mr. Collins to take his leave, but he continued stubbornly to sit and wait for more news.

"I sent a note to Lady Catherine, to be certain."

"Mr. Darcy asked to deliver the news personally," Charlotte said.

"Yes, and he shall. And you and Miss Elizabeth will be as sisters."

"Cousins," Elizabeth said, dryly.

Mr. Collins was far more the social climber than Elizabeth was, though society would see no such thing. Elizabeth doubted Lady Catherine would receive the 'good news' with much cheer. Pure fury seemed more likely.

Lady Catherine had no wish to form a familial relationship with Mr. Collins or any Bennet, Elizabeth surmised. If Mr. Collins had an ounce of sense, which evidence had proven repeatedly he lacked, he would have allowed Mr. Darcy to endure this revelation and not be so transparent in his glee at his own rise in circumstances.

Alas.

Any hope Elizabeth had of averting the prior morning's disaster had faded.

"It is so exciting that we will have a wedding." He flapped his hands as he talked, and Elizabeth thought he must have turned into a duck on his trip back to the parsonage, but that comparison would insult the duck.

"He said he would tell her himself," Elizabeth said, her voice low. "Why could you not wait for him to do that?"

"I only sent a very short note; he will still have plenty to tell."

Elizabeth looked at him over her tea. If she could get away with strangling him, she would. However, those thoughts did nothing to solve the problem. Now, she had to contend with Lady Catherine. Well, that would happen anyway.

Mr. Collins said, "You have done so much better than I thought you would, dear cousin. Had I known Mr. Darcy was in your sights, I would have better understood why you turned down my offer." Mr. Collins continued to babble with little care for those around him which proved fortunate for Elizabeth. She did not know whether to be offended by his last remark or to laugh at him.

"Have you two been courting?" Mr. Collins asked the question she least wanted to hear. She needed to continue Mr. Darcy's lie.

"Not exactly. We have met on occasion, but he revealed to me that his feelings for me were quite ardent, and I realized that my feelings were as fervent." Mr. Collins was nodding and smiling.

"That is so lovely," Charlotte exclaimed before her husband could say more. "To think, you told me you found him aloof! It is clear your feelings have changed."

"Yes," Elizabeth looked at her friend with gratitude. She had stopped her husband from continuing his grasping and vaguely insulting diatribe. "I have learned more about Mr. Darcy, and in some areas, I have learned that I was naïve, nay gullible about situations presented to me." She smiled again, and this time it was less forced.

There was a knock at the sitting-room door, and the butler entered with a salver holding an envelope. "A note from Lady Catherine de Bourgh for Miss Bennet," he announced walking towards Elizabeth.

"Oh my," Elizabeth mumbled more to herself than to anyone in the room. "Lady Catherine wishes to receive me. Immediately." Elizabeth knew that Lady Catherine de Bourgh did not care for her beyond the level of well-dressed country maid, but then, to Lady Catherine, all except a select few were beneath her.

Elizabeth had eaten enough dinners with Lady Catherine since she had been visiting Charlotte to realize that criticism was her best attempt at kindness. How would she react to her favorite nephew, and therefore a man of means worth recognizing as a person of importance, marrying below his station instead of marrying her daughter, Miss Anne de

Bourgh? She could not be pleased and would want to let that fact be known.

"Oh come now," Mr. Collins said, "she only wishes to congratulate you in person." Elizabeth could think of several things Lady de Bourgh might want to do, and none of them had anything to do with well wishes and congratulatory felicitations.

"If you like, Charlotte and I could come with you."

Elizabeth gave him her best smile, "I am sorry, but the note requests my presence alone."

Mr. Collins looked crestfallen; he never missed an opportunity to be in Lady Catherine's company. In one respect, Elizabeth was glad Lady Catherine had not invited Mr. Collins. Elizabeth did not relish being berated in front of witnesses, especially her cousin. He would spread rumor as fast as the crow flies in summer, and she did not need that type of notoriety.

On the other hand, Elizabeth was unnerved to face Lady Catherine alone as even in company she could try one's mettle. With no one to stand with her, Elizabeth would have to face her alone, as she suspected anger and wrath would be the lady's only companions. She would think only the worst of Elizabeth.

"Lady Catherine de Bourgh has sent her carriage." Elizabeth would have preferred to walk, if only to sort her thoughts, but she could not reject Lady Catherine's carriage. "I must go," Elizabeth said, taking a final sip of her now lukewarm tea.

CHAPTER 9

"You trapped my nephew," Lady Catherine de Bourgh snarled. "Now, my question is, how much will it take for you to disappear?"

Elizabeth had barely sat down in Lady Catherine's drawing room and was taken aback by the directness of her accusation. "I did no such thing, Lady de Bourgh. I am offended that you would think so poorly of my character, and that this is all about money. In fact, money plays a very minor part in this if at all, and I am appalled that you reach that conclusion without even talking me."

"This note from Mr. Collins, who is of good character and having no reason to lie, says that he came upon you two in the forest, unchaperoned and you were in dishabille in his arms. What am I supposed to think? You trapped my nephew by appealing to his manly nature with your feminine wiles. I want to know how much I need to pay to get you to go away. I have ordered my coachman to take you anywhere you wish to go, as long as it is not Rosings or Pemberley."

Elizabeth's cheeks reddened, and she felt short of breath. Nothing she said would change the old woman's mind either.

Listen to her. Elizabeth remembered Charlotte's advice and unfolded her hands which had been in her lap. *But do not accede everything.* "With all due respect, you do not understand the full situation, Lady Catherine. Perhaps, you might take the time to talk to Mr. Darcy about what happened, before you accuse me of ill intent. There was no entrapment intended."

"Why should I believe you? Ladies of your sort seek to improve their lot by trapping wealthy gentlemen like Mr. Darcy. You are not a young woman, Miss Bennet, and Mr. Darcy would be a fine catch for you. You would restore your family coffers, avoid spinsterhood and live a life of luxury. I did not believe you a loose woman, but your behavior begs otherwise."

"This is not about money," Elizabeth snapped at her, then closed her eyes and took a deep breath.

"It is always about the money, and as you bring neither dowry nor station to this marriage, what am I to think? Your estate is entailed to Mr. Collins. If you do not marry a man of some means, you are destitute. You are not the first woman to use her charms to improve her station."

"You think so little of me that you would accuse me of entrapment for monetary gain?"

"What else am I to think? I know my nephew does not have a deep affection for you; he is too much of a gentleman to not do the honorable thing when you were caught."

"Obviously, you do not know everything about your nephew, or this news would not be such a surprise."

"Mind your tongue, girl. He is to marry my daughter who has impeccable standing and is above reproach. You threw yourself at my nephew, used your feminine artifices and engineered a compromising situation with your cousin as a witness."

"You know nothing of our relationship or our feelings," Elizabeth's voice raised as she leaned closer to Lady de Bourgh. She took a breath, lowering her eyes and admonishing herself to have patience. *Avoid arguing with her.*

Lady Catherine said, "I know enough to know that you set this up, that you provoked him and laid out your charms to rile his feelings, so he forgot self-control and propriety in the situation. It is a woman's duty to keep a man in check. Let me say that you failed, and I can only conclude that it was deliberate. This will be remedied."

Did he do the honorable thing? Had their kiss been but a dalliance on his part? Did her lack of self-control cause her ruin? Elizabeth could not believe that about him, as he had seemed sincere in his feelings. Knowing Mr. Darcy's loathing of subterfuge, he would not engage in such behavior wanting only a bit of fun or worse still, a mistress.

"Mr. Darcy is an honorable man and a gentleman. His attentions to me are sincere."

"Sincere," Lady Catherine scoffed, "my nephew got caught up in your web of desire, one you planned and executed."

"You are so used to conspiracies, you can only assume this is another. We have been working towards an understanding. I know you refuse to see that, but it is fact and not a fiction or web contrived by me." As Elizabeth replied to her, doubts and cautions assailed her mind unbidden. *What if Lady Catherine's words are true? What then?*

"How dare you speak to me in such a manner!" Lady Catherine countered. "I am well acquainted with low women. My nephew will not marry you."

Elizabeth took a deep breath before continuing. "Is Mr. Darcy here? Perhaps he can tell me himself that he does not wish to marry me?"

"You do not request an audience with my nephew. Should he wish to speak with you, I shall inform you of when and how."

Elizabeth needed to regain her composure. All the days of criticism from this woman that she had tolerated for Charlotte's sake wore on her nerves. "Is there anything else you wish to tell me?"

Elizabeth wanted to be anywhere but in Lady Catherine de Bourgh's private drawing room.

"I want you out of Hunsford. If you will not accept my generous offer, so be it."

"Mr. Darcy and I are to wed."

"Mr. Darcy is not here. He has made no announcement. You are mistaken."

"He left for a Special License." Elizabeth had to believe that. Even if Mr. Darcy had only offered from a sense of duty, he would not betray his honor. He would at least speak with her first.

"I have instructed Mr. Collins to say nothing of what happened. Your virtue, such as it is, will be spared. And out of Christian charity, my carriage will take you anywhere you choose. But I want you away from my nephew. I will send a note to Mr. Collins to have your things sent where ever you wish."

"Excuse me?" Lady Catherine's last words shocked. "You will have me leave without saying goodbye?"

"You should have thought of that before you tried to ruin my nephew's reputation and standing."

"Lady Catherine, you are a rude, conniving woman," Elizabeth countered. "And you cannot stop me from getting my belongings and saying goodbye."

Lady Catherine smiled at her. "I already have, my dear. The note I sent to Mr. and Mrs. Collins said your farewells, and I informed Mr. Collins that he and his wife are not to allow you return to the parsonage. Mr. Collins dare not cross my will in this, or anything, as you are well aware."

A parson with any spine might cross Lady Catherine de Bourgh, not that anyone would accuse Mr. Collins of possessing such.

"Should you persist, I shall rescind my offer of a

ride, and Mr. Collins will not allow you into the parsonage in either case. You will not get your things, or your monies, and you will walk where ever you want with the clothes on your back. If you believe Mr. Collins will defy my will, you are mistaken. He knows if he crosses me, I will make his life a misery. His and his lovely wife's."

Lady Catherine was correct. She might not have the power to see him removed from the parsonage, but she held the upper hand in their relationship. Mr. Collins was ruled not merely by ambition but also adoration of Lady Catherine. He would do as she asked. With ill-disguised joy, considering Elizabeth had rejected him once.

Lady Catherine had trapped her, for now. Elizabeth had to do as the lady wished until she could contact Mr. Darcy and find out for certain how things stood between them.

If things stood between them.

Elizabeth's best chance was to go to her uncle and aunt in London. It would be the easiest place for Mr. Darcy to find her, and she would be safe. "Your carriage can take me to Town," Elizabeth replied. "To my aunt and uncle's."

"Acceptable. Go then and never darken my door again. I wish I could say, go with God, but I cannot. After what you have done, you are not worthy of God's grace."

Elizabeth's cheeks reddened, but she did not reward Lady Catherine with seeing her cry. With her back straight and head held high, Elizabeth left.

Hopefully, Mr. Darcy would come for her and make things right. She was a fool to hope for such things. He had never admitted to love.

The coachman who handed her into the carriage was unfamiliar to Elizabeth, but she was so glad to leave the hateful woman's presence, she did not care. She settled herself in the carriage alone and started to cry. The day had started off so well, happy and full of promise. Now she was being whisked away from Mr. Darcy, and would need to explain to her aunt and uncle as much as she dared about her situation.

She had always held a fondness for her relatives, and they for her. She would impose upon her uncle to send an express to Mr. Darcy informing him of her location. Elizabeth could only pray that it was not intercepted at Rosings; she would also send an express to Charlotte who she surmised would be beside herself with worry.

CHAPTER 10

"What do you mean, she left?" Mr. Darcy was nearly shouting as he stood in the middle of the parsonage's drawing room. On his uncle's name, he had received an audience with the Archbishop that morning and, Special License in hand had returned to make a proper proposal.

Now, Elizabeth was gone.

Gone!

Breath catching at the shocking news, he took a moment to calm himself. *Why had Elizabeth left? Had she run from their situation when it was nearly resolved? Did she have second thoughts about their alliance?*

Was she willing to ruin herself to avoid marrying him?

It made no sense.

Darcy asked, "Where did Miss Elizabeth go?"

Mr. Collins waved his arms, sputtering and trying to explain. "Elizabeth left suddenly for Town to visit with her aunt and uncle."

While he was in Town acquiring the special license, she had run off to London, for what purpose?

"We are sending her belongings to them," Mrs. Collins interjected. Looking into her eyes, Mr. Darcy could see that she wished to say more but was hampered by her husband.

"And your sister, Mrs. Collins?" Mr. Darcy asked.

"*Miss Lucas* is welcome to stay," Mr. Collins interjected.

This implied Elizabeth had been unwelcome. Darcy saw red. "You forced Miss Elizabeth to leave?"

"No! Never! It is quite odd," Mr. Collins continued. "She went out and did not return."

Mr. Darcy looked from one to the other. "Where, pray tell, did she go?" He watched Mr. Collins gaze shift to his wife then back to him. *Something is wrong*, Darcy thought. *Something Mr. Collins seems reluctant to divulge. Did Elizabeth board a post to London without telling him? Why would she do that?*

His heart ached with the obvious conclusion. She was running away from him, so fast that she did not even stop in to pick up her things. What had he done to merit such treatment? *Yes, she was upset and overwhelmed at the sudden quickening pace of things, but to leave without an explanation of any sort?* He took a deep breath before continuing. "She went to London?"

Mr. Collins quickly agreed. "She was upset when she left, was she not, my dear Charlotte?"

"Yes, but Elizabeth is not the sort suddenly to run off. If she left," Charlotte ignored Mr. Collins' warning look and continued on quickly, "something must have occurred during her visit with Lady Catherine."

"Charlotte!"

"Miss Elizabeth visited my aunt?" Mr. Darcy responded to this new intelligence with a frown. "And after, she did not return." Anger rose in him anew. *What did his aunt say or do to cause Elizabeth to run?*

"Yes," Charlotte said. "We received notice to have her things sent to Town, is that not correct Mr. Collins?" She turned to look at her husband whose cheeks had turned beet red, a contrast to his normally wan countenance.

Mr. Collins huffed and spluttered in his

response, "Yes, yes, I was just getting to that part of the explanation."

Mr. Collins prevaricated, but the reason eluded Mr. Darcy. He addressed Mr. Collins carefully, although he wanted to grab the man and throttle the truth out of him. "How did you find out that Elizabeth's belongings needed to be shipped to London?"

"Find out?" Mr. Collins spluttered. "Pray, I received a note from Lady Catherine instructing, no uh, requesting Elizabeth's possessions sent to Town."

Darcy's mind swirled. *What had his aunt said to get Elizabeth to leave?* It could not have been a favorable discussion, and knowing his aunt as he did, she had torn into Elizabeth with the vicious streak he knew his aunt possessed. There could be no other reason for Elizabeth's sudden departure.

"What is odd," Mrs. Collins said so quietly that Darcy moved closer to understand her, "is that she did not return to even gather her monies. I asked my husband about this, as she also departed without retrieving some things I know were very dear to her heart. Personal things that ladies acquire over time and hold most dear, received from others they hold close, things like that."

Mrs. Collins' steady gaze told Mr. Darcy she was talking about a few things she knew Elizabeth and he shared.

How could she leave without taking her treasured possessions? Did she think so little of the expanding nature of their understanding? No, that couldn't be true.

Darcy could not believe that Elizabeth thought so little of his feelings that she would go without an explanation. And, with what Mrs. Collins was inferring, she did not believe that Elizabeth had left in that manner either. *He would have a word with his aunt, because therein lay the truth,* Darcy surmised. And, if he had to wring her neck to get the truth from her, he would. Or, at least he would threaten it to get the intelligence he needed.

"Thank you for your insights in this matter. I shall speak with my aunt." Mr. Darcy bowed. "I wish you both a good afternoon."

Turning on his heel to leave, slowing only for the customary responses from the Collins', he departed for his aunt's home.

CHAPTER 11

The rocking of the carriage and the drawn shades gave Elizabeth the feeling that she was in her own world, the outside blew asunder on its own axis. The trip to London was long, not as lengthy as the trip to Longbourn, but this road was choppier than she recalled.

Elizabeth was so upset at the start of the carriage ride, from all that had been said, she hardly noticed. Now that she had calmed her nerves, and the carriage continued, she noted the differences. Not a veteran traveler, Elizabeth wasn't ready to question the coachman's sense of direction, so she had to trust that the closer they came to London, the better the road would be.

Elizabeth's mind went back to the disagreeable conversation she had with Lady Catherine. To threaten Mr. Collins and Charlotte! The woman was despicable!

Lady Catherine's tirade showed that truth to Elizabeth.

The carriage ride made clear another, more troubling truth. Elizabeth's affections for Mr. Darcy were true. She wanted to marry him.

Not that such an outcome was likely at this point. Perhaps she could have her uncle post him a letter? Not to Lady Catherine's, but his estate was in Derbyshire. Lady Catherine had extolled its virtues enough. Pemberley. That is what they called it.

Elizabeth thought of her and Mr. Darcy's closeness – just this morning – before Mr. Collins interrupted them. Her thoughts had been askew, but one revelation stood out and even in remembrances lingered.

My feelings are stronger than simple admiration. It may be love. Mr. Darcy has offered to marry me, and if it is not obligation as he maintains, then I may have all I have ever wanted.

If they still had a chance.

Where Elizabeth had been confounded, she was

now resolute. If Mr. Darcy's opinion of her remained favorable, she would do her best to trust his love and her own. She fell asleep on that thought, his handsome smile and warm dark gaze foremost in her mind.

CHAPTER 12

Under normal circumstances, Mr. Darcy had patience with his aunt. He sat through her tirades about one piece of society gossip or another, or her condescension of the servants, the abhorrent state of the grounds or some supposed slight in her life.

These were not normal circumstances, and after waiting nearly an intolerable period for his aunt to appear, after she finished tending to her dressing and toilette activities, Mr. Darcy was at his wits end. When she appeared in her drawing room – the throne room as Mr. Darcy and Mr. Fitzwilliam, his cousin liked to quip – he was not ready for any kind of small talk.

"Aunt, why is Elizabeth in London? What did you say to her?" Mr. Darcy paced as he spoke.

"My dear nephew, sit down. Have you forgotten your manners?" Lady Catherine's smile was sanguine. "We are civil people, and we must maintain decorum. Is this how you address your poor aunt?"

Mr. Darcy took a deep breath and addressed her again. "I am to the point and will brook no less in return. What did you say to Miss Elizabeth Bennet to make her leave so suddenly?"

His aunt waved a handkerchief at her face like a fan, and his patience, already at its limit, was pushed even farther.

"If you must know, I reminded her of her station in life, gave her a sizable amount of money and sent her on her way to her relatives in London. She will not trouble you again, and there is no engagement or marriage besides that to my lovely daughter, Anne. As I have told you on over one occasion, women of her ilk are mercenary, and —"

Darcy had not meant to lay a hand on his aunt, but he grabbed her arm at the elbow. "You will tell me what you said to her, before you sent her on her way without allowing her to collect her things."

"Unhand me," Lady Catherine bellowed, loud

enough for the footman outside her drawing room to hear. "You will not treat me in this manner." The door opened making a soft swishing noise, and the footman peeked inside.

Seeing Mr. Darcy gripping Lady Catherine's arm, he inquired of them quietly, "Is there a problem?"

"No," Darcy barked.

"Yes," Lady Catherine bellowed.

"It is family business," Mr. Darcy breathed deeply to regain his composure while backing away from his aunt.

"Lady Catherine."

She lifted a hand, waving him away. "Fitzwilliam, you will behave."

Darcy breathed again. He gained nothing from terrorizing his aunt. He needed her cooperation to find Elizabeth.

The footman, seeing civility regained, stepped out. He had never seen Mr. Darcy so angry. Lady Catherine had pushed things too far, and he was sure her rough treatment was tied to the screaming fit she had with that young lady who left in tears earlier. That too was none of his concern, although all of it would become the stuff of gossip. Lady Catherine's rants and tirades often brought on whispering amongst the servant class as she was such a disagreeable mistress.

When Mr. Darcy looked into his aunt's eyes, he saw fear. *Good, she would answer his questions and stop with the games.* "You sent her by coach to London?"

Rubbing her elbow and shoulder, "I did. I thought you would be glad to get out of this compromised marriage proposal. You are free to marry dear Anne." Her voice was more of a whine at this point than the ferocious lioness roar she usually postured. "You hurt me." She rubbed her elbow. Her eyes shone with tears, but Mr. Darcy held little belief in their veracity. She said, "I only wanted to help you."

"You only wished to help yourself, and maybe Anne, but not me... Never me. It has always been about you, your wants, your demands. This time, my dear aunt, you have gone too far. Know this as truth: I will not marry your daughter, not because she is a disagreeable woman, but because I hold no affection for her beyond familial ties. I will marry Miss Elizabeth Bennet, if she will have me, after all you have done."

"I offered a reward, and she took it. Think what you will of me, you should not allow a handsome face and womanly form to turn you from all you love. It is foolishness!

"You will ruin our name. And for what? A social climber who has inflamed your lust to overwhelm your good sense? You will be a laughingstock! All of us will be laughingstocks." A tear rolled down her cheek. Darcy believed she was crying for herself, and perhaps her daughter, but mainly herself. Lady Catherine would not be mocked. "And you will make things hard for your sister, Georgiana. Think of her."

Darcy had not thought of his sister, and Lady Catherine's admonition caused him a moment's doubt. But marrying Elizabeth would erase any stain their compromise might bring.

Firm in his resolve, Darcy said, "I will marry Miss Elizabeth Bennet, if she will have me after this."

"I only did this because I am cognizant of how a decision made when you are young can haunt you for the rest of your days. Your Elizabeth Bennet is a woman of loose morals and low standing. Pray, I beg you to see how fast she took my offer of remuneration. She means you no good, only ill and you will find her unreceptive to your entreaties now that she has been paid. Then you will come back and tell me of the rightness of my cause on your behalf."

Mr. Darcy was at a loss how to respond. His aunt seemed too sincere in her story. For all her faults, she did not lie. Or at least, she had never lied to him. But Darcy also knew the depths she would go to get what she wanted. *If Aunt Catherine offered you money, why did you accept it, Elizabeth? I would have given you the world. But, his aunt had the title, but not that much in coin, did she not? Or had Elizabeth settled for almost nothing to get away from his aunt and him?*

Darcy's heart ached at the thought Elizabeth did not want to be with him and would risk ruin to herself and her family in rejecting him.

Darcy sighed. He would get no more from his aunt beyond more questions. For answers, he would have to ask Elizabeth herself.

Darcy said, "I bid you adieu, before I lose my temper further. Pray I find Elizabeth and all is well." He did a perfect bow leaving the drawing room.

"Fitzwilliam!" his aunt called, but he ignored her cries.

CHAPTER 13

The carriage rocked to a stop, waking Elizabeth.

They were not yet in London? Had something happened?

From the quiet within the carriage, Elizabeth knew they had not yet arrived in Town. Even during quiet periods, there was always an undertone of activity in the city. All she could hear was crickets and tree branches rustling in the wind. She sat up from her slumbering position, opening the shade closest to her, and all she saw was darkness and trees. Her stomach lurched, and she felt fear at the reality of where she was. *But, where was she?*

The door to the carriage opened and a big, burly man with a beard, smelling distinctly of fish gave her a snaggle-toothed grin leaned into the carriage. "So, missy, you are the extra special package I'm supposed to deliver to Lord Bee, am I? Get down out of there. I'll not hurt you, as long as you do as I say."

"What is going on? Who is Lord Bee?" Elizabeth trembled, her heart pounding in her ears. "I was supposed to go to my aunt and uncle in London. There has been some kind of mistake."

"No mistake, missy, I received instructions from his Lordship's solicitor that you were to be delivered to Lord Bee. Do not make me get up in this carriage and drag you out. We can do this hard way or the easy way. I like the latter because I get paid less if you are damaged."

This could not be real. This was some fevered nightmare that she hoped to wake up from soon. Her heart pounded, and she felt faint from the situation presented. *I will wake up soon. I will wake up soon.*

"What's it to be, missy? Easy or hard?"

Elizabeth took a deep breath and scrambled down from the carriage. *Lord Bee? Who was Lord Bee? Oh, Mr. Darcy, where are you?*

"You can call me Bart. It 'ent my given name, and you had best not call for me too often, understand? I will make you ready for Lord Bee. The rules are simple," he said as he led her up to a small cabin in a clearing in the woods. Smoke rose from the chimney, and when he unlocked the door, smells of meat and potatoes wafted her way. "You stay where I put you, and you don't run. My wife will be back shortly; her name is Willow, and she answers to me. Do you understand me?"

"Yes," Elizabeth whispered. "When can I go to my aunt and uncle's?" She felt a pang of hope; however, Bart dashed it.

"You belong to my master now, Lord Bee. He will be taking you on a long voyage to India, and you will be one of his to do with as he likes. I have nothing to do with that; I just need to feed you, keep you, and prepare you for the journey." Tears slid down her cheeks. *What horror was this?*

Had Lady Catherine done all of this to keep her nephew from marrying her? She would become the slave of Lord Bee and go to India? No! She would not. *Would Mr. Darcy be able to find me in such a far-off land? Will Mr. Darcy still love me when he finds me?*

The door opened and a thin woman came in carrying a little boy of about six. His arm was bandaged and his head had a big lump on it. "This be Willow, my wife. This is," he pulled a piece of paper out of his pocket and addressed his wife,

"Elizabeth." The woman inclined her head and placed her little boy on the cabin floor.

"We are not bad people," Bart rambled on, "we just need the money to get our boy's leg taken care of or he will walk with a limp for the rest of his days."

Elizabeth began to relax seeing that these two people were not evil for evil's sake, and while she kept her guard up somewhat, she did not think herself in imminent danger. Willow invited her to sit at the table, and the little boy walked near her, but stayed just out of her reach. He had been instructed to not trust strangers which went against how most children his age acted. Elizabeth noted that for future reference.

Perhaps engaging in conversation would make them relax and give her a chance to run. She was still wearing her good boots. "What is his name?" Elizabeth asked smiling.

"Alban," Willow replied. "Named after me father." Her gaze kept sliding away from Elizabeth, which made her uneasy.

"Very fine," Elizabeth replied, gazing with what she hoped looked like idle curiosity around the cabin. Bart watched her, and as the food was being served, he went to the root cellar and returned with some rope.

"Take off your boots, missy. We can't have you running' off now." He made a loop with the rope, kicked her shoes away and pulled it taut on her ankle. "That ought to hold ya." The rope itched, and Elizabeth knew it would start chaffing after a while, but that seemed the least of her worries. She couldn't run without shoes, and how would she get out of the rope? Interrupting her reverie, Willow gave her a wooden bowl and some stew.

"We eat well," Bart said conversationally, "when one of you comes through here. Meat, potatoes and vegetables." He grinned at Elizabeth, although Willow did not join in to the conversation or even smile. She gave her son some stew out of the same bowl she was eating from, and as hard as Elizabeth tried, she could not catch her eye.

Elizabeth was not the first one they had done this to. Elizabeth took a taste of the food; it was delicious, but there was a knot in the pit of her stomach. Bart showed no such qualms to dampen his appetite, and after much slurping, he let out a loud burp, patting his paunchy stomach. Willow ate a small amount, as did her son, but she didn't seem to have an appetite for food either.

"You are not hungry, miss?" Bart asked after a pause.

"No, not really," Elizabeth replied lowering her gaze to her lap. She folded her hands out of habit and waited for the next event.

"That be a shame, missy, as what I need to do next is unpleasant. Eat."

Elizabeth's gaze shot up in fear. *Unpleasant? What could be more unpleasant than being kidnapped, taken to God only knows where and being tied by the ankle like chattel?*

It would be prudent to stay quiet, but Elizabeth would not submit without a fight. If she knew what would happen, she could prepare herself. It was a small measure of control over her life at this point. She took a deep breath before asking, "What could be more unpleasant than what you have already done to me?"

Bart stared at her, blank faced. At first, Elizabeth thought he might assault her for her impertinence, but then he guffawed, holding his stomach with the mirth he felt. "I guess ye be right, then."

Elizabeth ate slowly. It did not matter. After another five minutes, Bart snatched the bowl away. "We need to get started."

Willow interceded, asking if they could put their son to bed first. "He need not see this."

Elizabeth's tears returned. As she feared, dinner had only been a respite in the nightmare. She gripped her hands together as Willow cleared the table. Bart took his son into the back room to put him down, and Willow cleaned the table placing the dishes aside for later cleaning.

She came over and sat in front of Elizabeth. "Do not scream. Do not run," she whispered. "It will only go worse for you, if you do. My husband has a wicked bad temper, although you wouldn't know it when he is in a good mood like now."

"Help me," Elizabeth whispered, but Willow got up and took the dishes outside, leaving Elizabeth alone in the eating area. She began to frantically work on the rope tied to her ankle. Pulling and tugging, she barely got it to move. She straightened her leg and started pulling at it until blood began to appear around it. Crying, she kept working. *It's only a little pain and blood.* She pulled and scraped as one then another fingernail split. Sweating from exertion and fear, Elizabeth was frantic; this might be her only chance to get away from these people. "Please, God help me," she whispered.

She froze as the door to the backroom opened and Bart returned. He either did not see or ignored the blood on her ankle.

"This part is unpleasant, and I will wait for Willow so we can start." He smiled down at her, his paunchy stomach just inches from her face.

Elizabeth considered biting him, but that would only buy her seconds, and with the rope on her ankle, she would have no time to get it off so she could run. The door to the outside opened, and Willow came back in holding the cleaned dishes. She put them on the side and came to stand next to her husband.

"Get the rest of the rope. I put it next to the root cellar door." Willow dutifully picked it up, came back and handed it to him and waited, while he tied Elizabeth to the chair. Her fear was in her throat; she would retch. *Mr. Darcy, she thought wildly, I am no longer confused. I love you. If I survive this, will you still love me?*

CHAPTER 14

I t was past nine when Mr. Darcy arrived at his London townhouse. He could not, with any politeness, pay call to a lady at her home after dark, as much as he might wish. Besides, if she was angry, which she had a right to be considering the liberties he had taken with her on their last walk, he would better make his explanations in the light of morning, after both had occasion to sleep.

Or perhaps he was a coward.

What if she despised him?

As the night progressed, Darcy tossed and turned beneath the duvet. His head pounded. His mother had been prone to the megrims, but he had not had one since he was a child.

Though Darcy knew himself correct in his decision to wait, especially as the hours advanced towards dawn, the twisting of Darcy's stomach and the acid at the back of his throat spoke to a mistake.

Surely, Elizabeth could not have turned against him?

His eyes shut, and he dreamed of cold and the creak of a chain. A scream caught in his throat as he sat, bolt upright, in the bed, sheets and duvet damp.

Gray light filtered through the windows. In Town, the gray could be dawn or midafternoon, depending on the movement of the fogs. Darcy woke, made his morning ablutions, and forced himself to eat before he made for the address, at just after nine, Mrs. Collins had given him for Elizabeth's aunt and uncle.

As Mr. Darcy rode up Gracechurch Street in Cheapside, the home of Elizabeth's aunt and uncle, the sky dripped.

A stout, gray-haired gentleman in a dark gray coat stood on the stoop.

"Mr. Edward Gardiner?"

The gentleman nodded.

"I am Fitzwilliam Darcy," Darcy said, bowing.

"Mr. Darcy?" Mr. Gardiner cocked his head, eyes narrowed. "I suppose this is about my niece."

"Perhaps we could speak inside."

Mr. Gardiner's back straightened. "Yes." He pushed open the door and led Mr. Darcy to a small, wallpapered sitting room.

A thin, elegantly dressed, middle-aged woman with rye brown curls beneath a thin white cap, stepped into the room. "Is there word of Elizabeth?"

"Elizabeth is not here?"

"This is Mr. Fitzwilliam Darcy," Mr. Gardiner said, his lowering at Darcy's last name. "My wife, Mrs. Amanda Gardiner."

"Mr. Darcy." Mrs. Gardiner's lips tightened.

"Where is Miss Elizabeth?"

Mrs. Gardiner said, "My niece's luggage arrived yesterday with a note from Parson William Collins, of Hunsford saying she was going ahead in a second carriage."

Darcy's sense of wrongness sharpened.

Mr. Gardiner said, "Perhaps she stayed overnight at a posting inn?"

"It is not so far from Hunsford to Town."

"Or there was an accident on the road."

"I saw no accident," Darcy said. Admittedly, he had left well after Elizabeth's departure. But if there had been an accident, she might have been offered a ride on a passing carriage and made her way to a posting inn. There could, as Mr. Gardiner suggested, be an innocent explanation.

Mr. Darcy's stomach, along with the light throb behind his temples, made a lie of his attempts at calm. And Mr. Gardiner had been concerned enough to be waiting by the door for his niece before Mr. Darcy's arrival.

"While we are grateful for your concern, Mr. Darcy," Mr. Gardiner cut into Darcy's thoughts. "What is your business with our niece? How are you... acquainted?" Again, the narrowed eyes. While he was not outright hostile, Mr. Gardiner had offered Mr. Darcy neither a seat nor refreshments.

Perhaps he knew something of Mr. Darcy and Elizabeth's compromise. If so, Darcy had best set the record straight of his intentions straightaway. "Your niece and I are to marry, if she will have me."

"It is true!" Mrs. Gardiner put a hand up to her mouth.

"Yes. I am in love with Miss Elizabeth. Not merely infatuated, I hold affections for your niece which far exceed what I can convey in words."

Mr. Gardiner cocked his head. "And my niece? She returns your affections?"

"I pray. Miss Elizabeth and I have grown closer these past weeks."

"Then why has Elizabeth chosen to pay a sudden call to us?"

"I do not know and can only assume she doubts me. I came to put her doubts to rest." But what if her doubts were not of his intentions but of her own? What if the signs of affection she had shown were not genuine? What if he had frightened her with his forwardness?

Honor and propriety demanded they marry, but what if she could not love him?

Darcy squeezed his eyes shut. Elizabeth had shown no signs of disgust. He had asked to kiss her, and she had said yes. Darcy knew enough to recognize a lady's interest.

The key issue was Elizabeth was missing.

Darcy said, "If Miss Elizabeth does not wish to marry, then I will withdraw my suit and do my best to quell what rumors may have already spread. What worries me is Miss Elizabeth has not arrived here. If she left at the noon hour, as the Collins' informed me, she should have arrived by yesterday evening.

"My aunt, Lady Catherine de Bourgh treated Miss Elizabeth horribly. Perhaps Miss Elizabeth was overwrought?" Not that Darcy could imagine such a thing of the self-possessed young lady. "I have set my aunt straight on all issues pursuant to my courting and marrying your niece. I know that our start to the engagement was less than ideal, but I am sworn on this course, and tell you with all sincerity that I adore and cherish Miss Elizabeth and will make her happy for the rest of my days."

Mr. Gardiner, his face grave, said, "None of this is like Elizabeth. Sudden courtships. Travel without clothing or monies. And now, she is vanished? My wife and I are afraid something terrible may have happened."

Mrs. Gardiner nodded. Her face was pale, eyes smudged beneath in purple-gray. "I have had the most terrible aching in my head," she said. "Since last night. Something is wrong."

Darcy, having experienced the same unease, nodded. "I believe something is wrong as well. By your leave, I want to help."

Mr. Gardiner sighed. "Though our families are not well acquainted, I have heard good things of the Darcys. We appreciate any help you can offer. Greatly."

Mrs. Gardiner rose. "In her baggage was a note from Mr. Collins, and concealed in her personal toilette case, a note from Mrs. Collins. I shall retrieve them."

Mrs. Gardiner left the drawing room, returning after a few moments with letters in hand.

Mr. Darcy took them, sat, and read:

MR. GARDINER,

It is with a heavy heart that I send Miss Elizabeth Bennet's belongs to you, because an unconscionable violation of propriety has occurred. My wife, Charlotte and I took a morning walk at the behest of our patroness, Lady Catherine de Bourgh, who had sent a note showing that walking was good for the constitution and fended off unnecessary pounds in my humble and loyal partner. While I had not taken notice of the extra pounds Charlotte had gained, I was immediately in agreement with Lady Catherine for the need for a constitu-tional every day for her sake.

When we came upon them, Mr. Darcy did the honorable and gentlemanly thing, stating that he was planning on marrying my cousin post haste. Mrs. Collins and I were, at first, overjoyed to hear of my dear cousin's engagement to Mr. Fitzwilliam Darcy, who is the nephew to Lady Catherine and Master of Pemberley. I am sure with this resume you must realize that he is of impeccable character and above reproach. We came upon this happy news as we discovered the two parties in a most compromising position in the groves near our home.

Imagine my shock when I sent a note to Lady Catherine of the joyous event and then came to find out it was a trap – mercenary and without feeling – set by your niece to trap poor Mr. Darcy into marrying her to increase her family coffers and establish herself in polite society as the Mistress of Pemberley.

Lady Catherine was beside herself and requested an audience with Miss Bennet to straighten things out. It would have been a grievous scandal without the timely intervention of our gracious and generous patron, Lady Catherine de Bourgh who sent her away with the money she wanted and her promise not to honor Mr. Darcy's proposal of marriage.

I have always wondered at the upbringing of my cousin, as she turned down a Christian and righteous proposal from myself, an obedient servant of God, to pursue financial gain even if it meant the ruination of her reputation. Now we know where her heart and mind dwells.

I wish you all the best, and hope that my letter finds you in good spirits.

Yours faithfully,

Mr. William Collins of Hunsford Parsonage

MR. DARCY GRIPPED THE NOTE, WHITE KNUCKLED

in his chair. *That pompous, sycophantic fool.* He gritted his teeth and said nothing, resisting the urge to ball the parchment up and toss it into the wastebasket. The next note was from Mrs. Collins:

DEAR MR. AND MRS. GARDINER,

I write this note because I am terribly worried about Elizabeth. While my husband and I caught Elizabeth and Mr. Darcy in a compromising position, I cannot help but think this cannot be the dastardly plot my husband suggests. Pray, keep that thought in mind as you read the rest of this note.

Elizabeth would not have left the way she did, unless she was without a choice. I will stake my friendship on this premise.

After the incident on the path, I had a private talk with Elizabeth prior to her being summoned to Lady Catherine's residence. While Elizabeth was taken aback by all that transpired and nervous to meet with Lady Catherine, she was not given to a fit of nerves that would escalate into sudden flight. Again, because of my long friendship with Elizabeth, I state unequivocally this knowledge to be true.

I am so worried about the state of my friend, that I will relay a confidence she shared with me prior to departing my home for her meeting. Elizabeth said she held a deep and abiding affection for Mr. Darcy, which surprised her considering their short acquaintanceship. Elizabeth had hoped things would take their natural course, and that there would be a favorable resolution for all parties involved.

Further, Elizabeth was more worried about how this would affect Mr. Darcy's life than her own, and was coming to an acceptance for the change in pace of matters between them.

It is my belief that no matter what transpired between Elizabeth and Lady Catherine, Elizabeth would never leave without an appearance or at least a note by this time. She is strong of will, and quite capable of weathering whatever storm leveled at her. Leaving behind possessions I know are dear to her is not in her nature, and she has always been very conscientious about her duties and civilities to all.

I state this opinion because of the years I have been her staunchest and closest friend. Besides her dearest sister Jane, I believe I know Elizabeth best. No matter what indignities Elizabeth may have suffered, she would not have gone without a note or a goodbye. She is practical, and would have come by for her belongs even though she was no longer welcome here per my husband.

Please, I beg of you, have Elizabeth send me a post as soon as she arrives. I am so worried for her well-being.

. . .

GOD BLESS YOU,

I remain,

Mrs. Charlotte Collins

AS MR. DARCY FINISHED THE SECOND LETTER, HE looked up at the expectant looks on the Gardiner's faces.

"Miss Elizabeth did not deceive me," Darcy said. "I know this." And he also knew they had to search for her. That sense of wrongness was only growing stronger. "We must find her."

Did he need to return to Rosings or start on this end and work his way backwards?

"We had thought she might have returned home and have sent a letter to Longbourn, their estate."

"Good." Darcy only prayed Elizabeth was there and safe. But prayers were not enough. "We shall spare no expense to ensure her safe return."

"And if she was abducted?" Mrs. Gardiner interjected. "I have heard stories of abductions near Hunsford."

Darcy thought of Richard and his discussion of the missing servant women. Elizabeth was not a servant, nor had she been walking. But if she had been robbed and injured?

Darcy's heart caught in his throat. "We must hope for the best. I will retrace her path. What can you do here?"

"I have some... *associates* on the docks who might be of help, if paid," Mr. Gardiner said.

Darcy nodded. "Allow me to write my solicitor's information for payment."

"Elizabeth is our niece, Mr. Darcy!"

"And my fiancée." If she would have him. "We will find her."

Darcy could not live with himself if he let Elizabeth slip away again.

CHAPTER 15

Days later, back in the Gardiner's drawing room, Darcy struggled to remain hopeful. He and Richard had questioned Lady Catherine's coachman who revealed the Lady had hired men and a carriage for Miss Elizabeth.

Lady Catherine herself had not been forthcoming about the details of Elizabeth's departure, which left Darcy, the Gardiners and the Bennets with little choice but to continue on their own.

Mr. Gardiner explained, "The search parties have found nothing. Neither in Town nor on the roads. Your aunt? The coachman?"

Darcy shook his head. "My cousin has been helping the neighboring parish constable to discover who might be abducting local servant women."

Mrs. Gardiner wrung her hands. "You believe someone abducted Elizabeth?"

"It does not fit. Elizabeth was not a servant. And the others..." It was too indelicate to suggest. "Many believe the maids ran off, considering. Miss Elizabeth had no such history."

"And if they made a mistake?"

Then where was Elizabeth now? Snatching maids of poor character was relatively safe, but to abduct a gentry lady? That put them in much greater danger. If they discovered their mistake, they might find it easier to dispatch with Elizabeth rather than free her and risk her exposing their identities.

Darcy shivered. No, he could not believe Elizabeth dead.

Perhaps Elizabeth had taken a fall and lay insensate with kind farmers. He could only pray. "My cousin, Colonel Richard Fitzwilliam, will arrive in Town this evening. He believes there may be some connection between the missing women and the London docks."

Mr. Gardiner nodded. "My associates have assured me they will inform me if they see Elizabeth. The miniature is a few years aged but a well enough likeness."

"They will help?" Was it not just as likely these criminals would warn their brethren as aid the Gardiners?

Mr. Gardiner said, "If another does not pay them more handsomely for their silence." He sighed. "I have also made it clear whoever informs us of her whereabouts will be handsomely rewarded if she is found, alive."

Mrs. Gardiner sobbed. "Lizzy! If she has—!"

"My dear." Mr. Gardiner took her hand. "We will find Lizzy. We must."

Darcy said, "Let us not assume the worst. She could be merely injured and unable to send a post."

"It has been days!"

"A blow to the head might have addled her, for a while." This was Darcy's best-case scenario. "Whatever happened, we cannot lose hope."

Mrs. Gardiner nodded. "Good. That will help mollify your sister. I have convinced her to stay at Longbourn, for now, in case Lizzy returns home."

Mr. Gardiner breathed a sigh of relief. "Forgive me, but I cannot imagine my sister would be of any help here. Her *nerves*, you understand."

Darcy's nerves were frayed as well. The dreams had only grown worse. Darkness. Fear. Painful thirst.

Were these dreams delusions brought forth by his fears or a true vision? It might be blasphemy to entertain the notion, but if they meant Elizabeth lived, he would accept this blasphemy as a gift.

Darcy said, "Tomorrow, with Richard, we should visit the docks again. For now, I shall call on my solicitor and see if his inquiries have born further fruit. Shall we reconvene in the morning?"

With good fortune, Richard would have some ideas of paths to pursue tonight. His military career and passion for pugilism gave him a wider variety of colorful acquaintances than Darcy had.

The Gardiners agreed.

COL. FITZWILLIAM WAS UNCHARACTERISTICALLY grim when he arrived at Darcy's townhouse at half past four.

"Miss Elizabeth?"

"No news as yet." Richard sighed. "Of Miss Bennet or the other missing women."

After instructing the footmen to see to Col. Fitzwilliam's luggage, Darcy led his cousin to the study for conversation and brandy.

Richard threw his back in one gulp. He swallowed. Shut his eyes. "Four women are missing, at least."

"You are including Elizabeth."

"All four left my hired carriage."

"I thought they had run off."

"That is what some believe, but the stable masters confirmed it. The carriages were hired, but from whom?" Richard shook his head. "Why? A poor maid cannot afford to hire a carriage to flee her employment."

"You believe Aunt Catherine—?" Darcy's breath caught.

No, his aunt wouldn't have Elizabeth kidnapped to break their engagement? The thought of his stiff, proper aunt hiring brigands to do away with her nephew's fiancée was laughable. How would Lady Catherine even find such thugs, let alone arrange an abduction in less than one day?

"Of course, I do not believe Aunt Catherine had anything to do with Miss Elizabeth's disappearance. She hired a carriage though. Perhaps Elizabeth's abduction was accidental?"

Except Lady Catherine had something to gain from Elizabeth's disappearance. She saw Elizabeth as the obstacle to Darcy and her daughter's marriage. Darcy had no affection for Anne or any intention of marrying her, but Aunt Catherine refused to see this.

Still, to imagine Aunt Catherine arranging a kidnapping was a ludicrous notion.

Richard said, "One of the stable hands at the post inn mentioned one of the footmen had a cockney accent. It is thin, but the only lead worth pursuing."

"Mr. Gardiner, Miss Elizabeth's uncle, suggests we search the docks."

Richard nodded. "There is an... *acquaintance* I hope to meet, this evening, and then I am at your disposal."

"Allow me to accompany you."

Richard looked Darcy up and down. "You will need shabbier clothes

"Richard, we have done this before."

Richard's lips twitched. "True."

RICHARD'S ACQUAINTANCE WAS A DRAB BROWN man, his only distinguishing feature, his left leg which had been amputated below the knee. Trouser leg was sewn shut, and a crutch leaned against the empty section of the bench at his side. He looked

up from a glass of ale as Richard and Darcy entered.

"Colonel." He started to stand as Richard approached, but Richard waved him to sit.

"Phillips," Richard said with a grin.

The man smiled with closed lips. He glanced over at Darcy before his gaze returned to Richard. "It has been a long time."

"Thank you for speaking with me."

A barmaid came and took their order. Richard made introductions and he and Edward Phillips shared war stories.

The drinks were served, and Phillips took a long swig. He sighed. "Messy business, these women."

"Have you learned something?" Darcy cut in. "Please. Miss Elizabeth is my fiancée."

Phillips looked at Richard, who said, "You can trust him as you do me."

"I looked into what you asked. Missing servant women." Phillips pressed his lips together. "It is not good news, sir. They are being shipped to India is what I heard. Been happening for some time, a year at least, out of Falmouth."

If Elizabeth had been abducted and sent from Falmouth, Darcy despaired of seeing her again.

Phillips explained, "Two escaped, but it is bad

business." He drank again. "They were branded, sir, like cattle. Brutalized. One took her own life. The parson, a good man, declared the death an accident so she could be buried... some lies are small sins, you understand. I am uncertain what happened to the other young woman. They say she went home to her family."

Darcy's heart ached. *Had Elizabeth gotten caught up in this nightmare? Was she mistaken for a maidservant and secreted away into this horror?* The very thought made him sick, but if he stood any chance of getting Elizabeth back, he would need to face this possibility.

"Falmouth then?" Darcy asked.

Phillips shook his head. "Like as not, if they are still in business, they are shipping from London. When the colonel wrote me he was looking into such cases, I asked around. My papa worked the docks. Hard work, but not all dishonest. No gentry toffs, present company excepted," he added, glancing at Mr. Darcy but not, oddly, Richard, "care what happens to young, servant girls. Especially those who have proved too tempting to a married gent."

Darcy swallowed. Hearing the words so plainly from Phillip's mouth made Darcy aware of his own guilt. He had felt only relief when discovering the missing women were servants. If Elizabeth were not involved, would Darcy be here now, investigating?

Richard said, "We care what happens."

"You are a good man, Colonel Fitzwilliam." Phillips wiped his thumb over the rim of the glass, now half-empty. "There are seven captains who might be involved. Four are bound for Bombay, scheduled to leave by the week's end." He reached into his jacket and pulled out a folded note. "You cannot say you got this from me, you understand. I have a wife and a daughter."

"You have my word," Richard said. He reached across the table and touched the top of Phillips' hand. "Thank you."

Phillips bowed his head. Swallowed. "The figuring you taught me, it saved us. I clerk now. Gives me some use and helps me and Mary. It is not the same as fighting, but..."

"Your help will save lives. That is more than some use, Phillips."

"By the grace of God, sir."

"To being of use." Richard raised his glass. They toasted. Drank.

Phillips finished his ale and rose, leaning on the table as he maneuvered his crutch under his arm.

They agreed to meet later that night, at the docks, with Mr. Gardiner.

Richard rose, bowed. Darcy followed.

Phillips ducked his head. "Colonel. Mr. Darcy."

Darcy paid the tab. Ale sloshed in his belly.

The vision of the woman screaming rose in Darcy's mind unbidden. If his beloved Elizabeth fell prey to this vile criminality, he would never forgive himself nor stop searching for her.

CHAPTER 16

Mr. Gardiner was waiting when Mr. Darcy arrived with Col. Fitzwilliam at his home the next morning. They sat in the breakfast nook over rolls and preserves with tea while they informed Mr. Gardiner on what Phillips had told him the night before.

Col. Fitzwilliam passed over the paper. "Can you help get us access to these ships?"

Mr. Gardiner nodded. "I suggest we keep this from my wife for now," Mr. Gardiner said, looking over his shoulder at the door. "If we find Elizabeth and they have brutalized her, time enough then to fill my wife's mind with the gruesome details. For now, let's just proceed hoping for the best."

Mr. Darcy agreed, although as more time

passed without a word from her, Darcy felt that the chances were good that Elizabeth had undergone some ordeal. Like Gardiner, he did not want to give up that shred of hope.

Over the course of the day, they scoured the docks, visiting each of the ships Phillips had listed in turn. Posing as potential passengers, Darcy and Richard gained access to the first. The second and third were not listed as passenger ships, though a purse full of gold allowed them access to one of the two. The crewmembers were Chinamen who called out to each other in their staccato, tonal speech. At Mr. Gardiner's inquiry, one replied in broken English, "No passenger."

An hour in nearby taverns made clear the crew kept to themselves, except for one who traded rice liquor for tobacco.

"He will be back before they ship off on Thursdee," one worker declared, wiping his hand beneath his chin to soak dribbles of ale into his beard. "Tomorrow, like as not."

After determining when and where the trade usually took place, and with a few more coins, they persuaded the dockworkers to inform their Chinese acquaintance to set up a trade the next afternoon.

Coming up last in their list of ships was the

Lady Banks, a private transport and West Indiaman.

"It has been sailing between Britain and India," Gardiner supplied the intelligence. "She's owned by a Lord Braithwaite, who is titled but some of his ships run with trade. It is unusual, but he is a very odd man."

"Lord Braithwaite?" Darcy murmured. The name was familiar. He and Aunt Catherine's husband had been friends. Darcy remembered meeting the man as a child, vaguely, a tall, bald gentleman who smelled of spices and tobacco.

The ties to trade alone ought to have kept Lady Catherine from maintaining the acquaintanceship after her husband had passed. But if she had not, and now Elizabeth was on this Lord Braithwaite's ship…?

A group of men stood on the bridge of the ship, and Mr. Gardiner raised his hand to wave. "Excuse me, sir!" He started to walk over to the gangplank to board, Darcy and Richard following. "If I may, a moment?"

A scruffy young man, lip cut and eye bruised, stepped in front of the plank. He gripped a broom in his right hand. The stick was pitted and stained. "What is your business here?"

"I would like to speak with the owner of this vessel," Mr. Gardiner smiled. "I have a proposition he would find most interesting."

"We are set for Bombay, sir, tomorrow at dawn. What business?"

"Imports and exports," Mr. Gardiner said.

"Of a delicate sort," Darcy added. "We would prefer to discuss this... in private."

The man's eyes widened. "Lord Bee does not conduct business on his ship."

Darcy could not breathe. This was the ship. Was Elizabeth on board? He wanted to call out her name, but if she was on board... he could not risk it. Not yet.

Mr. Gardiner's asked. "Then where might we find him?"

The man shrugged, then called up to the bridge. "Captain! Gentlemen asking to speak to Lord Bee."

"He 'ent here."

"I know he 'ent!" The man turned back to them. He froze, fingers clenching on his broom, then, looking over Darcy's shoulder, jerked his chin to the side.

Darcy looked back.

On the dock, too far away to recognize more

than their forms, a dark-haired boy shuffled, flanked between two burly men. There was something familiar about the boy in the way he carried himself. Darcy started back down the gangplank.

Richard looked back. "Darcy?"

Thirst. Darcy's head ached.

Heart pounding, Darcy broke into a run towards the boy.

The boy was tall and too thin, his trousers reaching just halfway down his calf, his shirt too large, belted by a rope at the waist. Seeing Darcy approach, one of the flanking men grabbed the boy by the shoulder and started pulling him back.

The boy's expression was blank, his full lips parted and shining with drool as he mumbled to himself.

Their eyes met. The boy shook his head violently and keened, a high-pitched cry.

"Quiet!" one man shouted.

Darcy dashed towards the boy. He could not take both men on his own. Richard might, but Darcy's skills with his fists were not so well practiced. But Darcy could not lose this boy. Hair shorn, eyes like night. A part of Darcy knew, but he could not bear accepting it.

Behind Darcy, shouting, a gunshot.

One of the men cursed. The other let go. They ran.

Darcy leaped on the boy, throwing his arms around him and shielding the fragile body with his own.

The body, shivering, fit well in his arms. Mingled with the stink of sweat and fish guts, her scent.

"Lizzy?" Darcy held her. "Lizzy, we found you. You are safe."

In his arms, Elizabeth shivered. Her cry became a whimper, then silence.

CHAPTER 17

"**I**s that Miss Elizabeth?" Richard asked. At his side, he gripped his pistol.

Darcy nodded.

Mr. Gardiner stood between them and the boat, his arms over his chest. Lady Banks' crew had pulled their gangplank, and a group of tough-looking deckhands stood, some with heavy sticks, others wielding kitchen knives, along the deck's edge, facing the dock.

"Elizabeth?" Darcy stared into her eyes. Her expression was disturbingly placid. Had she been hurt in the fall?

Despite her poor clothing, Elizabeth's hands were soft. She fiddled with Darcy's fingers, an action that he had seen Elizabeth do from time to time with her own hands when she was nervous.

Not nervous. Terrified.

"We must get her away from here. Somewhere safe."

What had they done to her? The confident, laughing woman he had fallen in love with was a shell.

"Go, take her," Richard ordered. "And get help. This ship must not leave port."

"If it is Lord Braithwaite's, we may not have leave to stop it. We have no evidence Elizabeth was bound for the Lady Banks."

"Elizabeth?" Darcy tried again. "Who did this to you?"

Silence.

"Please, say something. Please!"

Silence.

Mr. Gardiner put a hand on Darcy's shoulder. "Come, Mr. Darcy, let us take my niece to safety."

As Mr. Gardiner knelt at Elizabeth's opposite side, Darcy loosened his grip, pushing Elizabeth to her uncle. Elizabeth whimpered and gripped his hands.

It was the most awareness Darcy had seen from her since she had cried out. He said, "I will carry her." With that, he lifted her. Elizabeth rested her head against his shoulder, her arms loosely around his body.

They left the dock area and made their way back onto the streets of London. Mr. Gardiner hailed a hackney cab, and the three of them piled in for the trip back to Mr. Gardiner's.

When they were in the cab, Mr. Gardiner stared at the ragged boy. Elizabeth. This was his niece. They had shorn her hair, and she stared, unseeing, her eyes smudged with dark circles beneath. She looked like someone who had been set adrift in a nightmare. He exchanged glances with Mr. Darcy who continued to hold Elizabeth despite propriety and good manners.

WHEN THEY ARRIVED AT THE GARDINER'S HOME in Cheapside, Mr. Gardiner jumped out of the cab, knocking on his front door frantically. Darcy was uncertain Elizabeth could stand, and he could not stand to let her go, so he carried her from the carriage into the house.

Darcy let Elizabeth down in the drawing room, on the sofa. She sat, staring as she gripped Darcy's hand.

"Come now Elizabeth, let us get you changed. And a bath."

Mrs. Gardiner bustled into the drawing room. "Lizzy!" Her smile froze and faded as she stared at the emaciated form of her niece in ragged boy's clothing. Lowering her voice, she went to Elizabeth's side and took her hand. "Lizzy? Are you hungry? Shall we get you some tea and an apple tart? I know how you love sweets."

A tear fell from Elizabeth's left eye. It ran a dirty trail down her cheek.

Rage flashed over Mrs. Gardiner's face. "Monsters. The devil take them for what they have done!"

Elizabeth flinched, shrinking away from her aunt.

"Oh, dear!" Mrs. Gardiner swallowed. "Poor dear, it is all to be well. I promise. Now, let us get you cleaned up. A nice, hot bath, that will be just the thing." Mrs. Gardiner chattered as she stood, putting her hands on Elizabeth's shoulders.

After a bit of coaxing, she got Elizabeth to stand.

Darcy stood with her.

"Mr. Darcy, I have it from here," Mrs. Gardiner said, her gaze flitting to his and Elizabeth's clasped hands.

Darcy said, "Miss Elizabeth, your aunt is here. You will have a lovely bath." He hated that he had to speak with her like a child or frightened animal. Whatever these men had done to her, Darcy would return it to them a thousand-fold. But he could not let his rage show. Not now.

Though it felt like he was severing a part of himself, Darcy let her hand go. Mrs. Gardiner slipped her arm around Elizabeth's waist and led her from the room.

CHAPTER 18

M rs. Gardiner took Elizabeth up the stairs, calling for her lady's maid, Becky, to assist with Elizabeth's bath.

While waiting for the bath, Mrs. Gardiner offered Elizabeth tarts, rolls, and fresh fruits, things that normally would have had her niece eating heartily.

But Elizabeth ignored the food. She ignored the chocolate and tea also, but grabbed at a glass of water the maid had added as an afterthought, gulping it down and cradling the glass.

"More," Mrs. Gardiner ordered.

After the second glass, Elizabeth withdrew again. The bath arrived.

As Becky and Mrs. Gardiner got the ragged

clothes off her, both women gasped in shock. Beneath layers of grime, bruises purpled Elizabeth's upper back and legs. Becky, a stout girl of seventeen-years, looked a bit green as she and Mrs. Gardiner lifted Elizabeth into the steaming water.

As the water darkened, both women worked to get the layers of dirt and mud off Elizabeth. "We may need a second bath," Mrs. Gardiner remarked. "Have them heat the water."

"Yes'm." Becky left and a minute later returned.

Even though her aunt made comforting tones and words, like she did when one of her children was sick, Elizabeth gave no response. She moved only when pulled this direction and that. Silent tears ran down her face.

"Come on, stand up now Miss Elizabeth," Becky said, getting behind Elizabeth. With a heave, she pulled Elizabeth to her feet. Mrs. Gardiner held out a linen robe to wrap her in. "Come on, love, just a short step," Mrs. Gardiner said, touching Elizabeth's leg.

Becky stepped back. Gasped. "Mrs. Gardiner!"

"What is it?"

Becky pointed, her finger shaking. "They branded her."

Mrs. Gardiner turned Elizabeth around.

Nausea churned. Mrs. Gardiner swallowed. On her lower back, just above her left buttock. Mrs. Gardiner brushed her fingers over the angry, raised skin.

Elizabeth screamed.

Mrs. Gardiner snatched her hand away as Elizabeth began to fight, spinning out of her aunt's reach, water sloshing as she flailed her arms.

Becky grabbed Elizabeth's arms so that Mrs. Gardiner would not get hit. "What have they done to her?" Becky sobbed holding on tight to her mistress.

Gently touching Elizabeth's cheeks, Mrs. Gardiner tried to calm her. "Shhhhh, shhhhh," she said again and again as if she were a young child. "Everything is fine, Lizzy. You are safe."

Elizabeth, gasping, whispered, "I have got to be quiet, or he will come again... be quiet... must be quiet."

Her aunt made comforting noises, achieving a calmative influence on her niece. Elizabeth stopped resisting, quietening and resuming a stare of resignation that broke her aunt's heart.

Both women were covered in water by the time they got Elizabeth out of the tub.

"Put her in the bed, Becky," Mrs. Gardiner ordered.

"But Miss Elizabeth's hair is still dirty, ma'am."

"We will wash it later. For now, let her sleep. And let me know when the apothecary is come. There must be something we can do for her mind."

Mrs. Gardiner hated the sight of her niece like this. Broken. She and Becky got Elizabeth into bed, pulling blankets up around her to warm her up. "My poor dear," Mrs. Gardiner's voice caught.

An hour later, the apothecary, Mr. Hill arrived.

Elizabeth appeared to have fallen asleep, but came alert and stiff when the doctor pulled at the covers.

"They branded her," Mrs. Gardiner explained. "She cannot abide it being touched."

Mr. Hill nodded. "We will need to keep the wound clean and watch for infection. You'll want to call for a surgeon if you want her bled."

Mrs. Gardiner hated the practice of bleeding though, having seen the effects on her youngest sister, Prudence, who had died when she was twelve. "Let us watch her," Mrs. Gardiner said. "She is already so weak."

"Hmmm." Mr. Hill placed his hand on Elizabeth's heart. "The beat is steady. She is too thin though. Laudanum for now. Sleep. It will allow her mind to heal." He gave the first dose in water. Elizabeth's eyes drooped and closed.

Mrs. Gardiner resolved to have hot broth and all of Elizabeth's favorites when she woke again. Just in case. The girl had shown no interest in food before, much to Mrs. Gardiner's dismay, only drinking water.

"This will help," Mrs. Gardiner said to Mr. Hill as he packed his bag to leave. "The laudanum? The draughts? Her mind will return?"

Mr. Hill sighed. "We can but do our best, but matters of the mind and heart are in the hands of God, Mrs. Gardiner."

Mrs. Gardiner nodded. Only when he turned his back did she allow her own tears to fall.

IN THE DRAWING ROOM, MRS. GARDINER SIPPED cold tea and related the details of Elizabeth's condition to her husband and Mr. Darcy. She spoke of the many bruises and lacerations on Elizabeth's body and whispered that Elizabeth had been branded.

"Branded?" Mr. Gardiner asked, eyes widening.

"Yes," Mrs. Gardiner replied, "branded with the letter B like one would cattle."

Mrs. Gardiner shook her head. "Who would have done such a thing?" she asked. "It is no wonder she is lost in her own mind."

Darcy said, "We will bring her back, Mrs. Gardiner." The pain of events was written across his countenance, and tears glistened at the edges of his eyes. It was as though, as Mrs. Gardiner described her niece's condition, Darcy felt every laceration, every bruise and indignity inflicted on his future wife.

"We will find who did this and see they hang," he said, looking at each of the Gardiners in turn. Though if the culprit was Lord Braithwaite, a noble of the Ton, justice would not be so easily served. Darcy could challenge him. Demand satisfaction. He was a fair shot, and the Good Lord would guide his hand, surely.

Whether it was Lord Braithwaite or someone else, Darcy would see they paid.

A footman announced Col. Fitzwilliam and led Richard into the drawing room.

"It is the devil's work." Col. Fitzwilliam blurted out, then bowed. "My apologies, Mr. and Mrs. Gardiner." He turned to Darcy. "Upon your departure, I sent a runner with a note to Sergeant Demmings, praying they have still assigned him to the Customs office, and begged for them to send someone to search Lord Braithwaite's boat. Lord Braithwaite's solicitor objected, but there was little he could do. And thank the heavens. Four women, in the cargo hold, shut up in a crate, by all that is holy! We would never have found them had one not reacted poorly to the drug and begun thrashing about."

Elizabeth had come within moments of the same fate. If Darcy had arrived earlier or later, they might never have known.

Richard started to pace. "Of course, the solicitor was *shocked*, and in his defense, he appeared so as he declared Lord Braithwaite certainly had nothing to do with such depravity."

"Were the other women... also branded?" Mrs. Gardiner asked.

Richard swallowed. "I had hoped Miss Elizabeth was spared that fate."

"Lord Braithwaite cannot get away with this," Darcy said. "No matter how he denies what happened, when Elizabeth awakens, we can call him before the Council of Lords and demand her rights."

Richard asked, "Has Miss Elizabeth told you anything of what happened to her?"

Mrs. Gardiner said, "She is asleep. Laudanum. Her mind... Mr. Hill says we must put it in the Lord's hands." She took a sip of her tea. "There is nothing we can do but wait, but and I can only hope time will rectify this."

Darcy could not believe Elizabeth was lost. Not forever. "We will get Miss Elizabeth back to herself. It may take time and patience." And love. Darcy promised love. "I am not going anywhere. My feelings have not changed, not one iota. If anything, my love has increased tenfold." Darcy tried to maintain his hope, but he had held that trembling waif of a woman who had been so full of life. She had lost weight, and looked sicklier than his cousin Anne. What had made such a severe impact on her mind and body.

Mr. Gardiner had said nothing up to that point. He looked ashen, pale; his lips were a thin line, and with each description his frown deepened. Never in his life had he encountered such wanton, vile evil. His own feelings for his niece made it impossible for him to say what he was thinking. He wanted the people who had done this to suffer, as his niece had suffered, and in the end, he wanted them all to die. He took another deep swig of his port, trying to quell the hatred he felt. Anybody who would do this to a young lady, to anyone in fact, was nothing, less than nothing.

To realize that such a level of evil existed in the world was too much to bear. And if Lord Braithwaite, a gentleman of the Ton, was responsible, Mr. Gardiner swore it would make no difference to his pursuit of justice.

Justice by his hand if not by the law.

This had been done deliberately to his niece and to other young ladies. No matter their station, it was evil. He wanted to see the men responsible hung, though hanging alone was too kind.

Mrs. Gardiner sensing her husband's distress leaned over and patted him on the arm. "It may not be Lord Braithwaite himself. We will find the people responsible," she said.

"Will you inform the Bennets, Mr. Gardiner?"

"Yes, but..." Mr. Gardiner glanced at his wife. "Perhaps it would be best to keep secret from her mother the full extent of her condition until she is more...recovered?"

"Your sister will not abide being apart from her daughter for long."

"Yes, of course. I simply meant...she and Lizzy are not as close."

"Lizzy and Jane are close enough, and Letitia is her mother. I will hear no more of this. If it was our daughter, would you wish to have such news kept from you?"

Mr. Gardiner sighed. "We shall, at the least, insist on Jane's presence."

Mrs. Gardiner nodded.

Darcy understood the family had to be informed, and he prayed their presence would bring Elizabeth back to him, but he could not help some resentment at having to share her.

When they married, he could care for her fully.

"She likes books," Darcy said. "I shall come every day and read to her."

Though such an offer was less than proper, Mr. Gardiner agreed. It was clear Mr. Darcy cared for his niece, and Mr. Gardiner would not deny the naked love in Mr. Darcy's eyes. Nor would he wish to. He was grateful for Mr. Darcy's obvious devotion.

They agreed upon the plan, and Mrs. Gardiner agreed to ask Jane to come ahead of the luggage. "Edward's sister has fragile nerves," she explained. "It is best if Jane arrives first."

Darcy stayed for a light dinner of cold bread, meat and cheeses. None ate with particular gusto.

Col. Fitzwilliam said, "I must take my leave."

Darcy, preferring to stay the night but having no polite way to insist, asked, "Before we take our leave, may I say goodnight to Miss Bennet?"

The Gardiners exchanged glances.

"Certainly," Mr. Gardiner said.

Mr. and Mrs. Gardiner smiled for the first time that evening.

"Of course, she will mostly likely be asleep." Mrs. Gardiner added. "She was administered laudanum."

"I will have my doctor over tomorrow morning," Darcy said.

"Not to bleed her!" Mrs. Gardiner held out her hand.

Darcy shook his head. "Merely for a second opinion. I believe Doctor Frederick Stanley the best in Town."

Mr. Gardiner nodded. "Thank you, sir."

A moment of normalcy in an abnormal situation.

They ascended to the upper floor together, and Mrs. Gardiner opened the door to Elizabeth's room, leaving the door open and allowing Mr. Darcy a few moments with Elizabeth.

Elizabeth slept, tossing and kicking at the duvet in distress, and sobbing. Mr. Darcy took her hand in his and whispered in her ear. "I am here, Lizzy. My beloved. You are safe now. Sleep. Just sleep." As he whispered, Elizabeth calmed.

Did she hear him?

"Sleep well. I will be back in the morning. All is well."

Darcy placed her hand on her stomach carefully, but when he went to let it go, her grip tightened. He squeezed her hand again.

"I am here. I will always be here." Her grip loosened, and she moaned again.

He stayed minutes longer, whispering entreaties and endearments.

"Darcy?" Richard whispered from the doorway.

Darcy was not a man prone to uncontrolled emotion, but seeing her like this and knowing he could not stay nearly broke him.

"I love you, Elizabeth. Come back to me." Darcy squeezed her hand one more time before he stood to join his cousin.

CHAPTER 19

Elizabeth sat in a small boat on a still pond tethered to a wooden dock. The tether was very long, and thus, the boat drifted to the middle. Mist obscured everything beyond the pond's banks and dock. Every direction she looked was mist, and because it shrouded everything, she felt safe.

No matter what had happened, Elizabeth could drift in her little boat at peace. Every now and again she heard: her voice, the voices of her captors, the voice of the little boy who poured water through the slats as she stood in the root cellar of a place she did not know.

But that was outside the mist.

Here, where she sat, there was no cellar, only Elizabeth in a small boat on a still pond.

It had been a long time since Elizabeth had seen anybody, and that was fine with her. With people came strangeness, pain and humiliation. She felt her head, and found a full length of tresses, not the short, chopped hair in the cellar. She felt her back where the brand had been, and it was gone.

Elizabeth had fought it. But she was too weak. The searing agony had sent her to darkness, and she had woken here.

A blessing. Elizabeth smiled.

Best of all, sometimes, at the dock, her beloved returned.

Elizabeth could not believe what Bart had told her: Mr. Darcy had sent her here because he did not wish to marry her. The thought made her ill, so she thought of something else, something nice like the flowers she could smell from beyond the fog.

"Where are you, my love?" No one answered.

Suddenly, the peace was stifling. Lonely.

Just silence. No bird song. No insect hummed. Even the lap of the water against her tiny boat was muffled.

Elizabeth waited.

Endless waiting.

But if she left, she would go back there.

Elizabeth looked at the dock and heard Mr. Darcy.

Fitzwilliam.

The pond was too far away to bind oneself in the chains of propriety.

Fitzwilliam whispered, at first too faint to hear. That was the way of the mist; it muffled everything. Before, she had accepted the muffled voices because the mist muffled all the horrors placed upon her person to a point where she could bear them.

But as time passed, her curiosity grew. He came and left, came and left. Sometimes, he spoke. Sometimes he sang. He was not an accomplished singer. Still, she wished to know why he came. What was Fitzwilliam so eager to tell her?

Was it him at all?

"Fitzwilliam Darcy," Bart laughed. "Mr. Fitzwilliam Darcy, the gent you compromised?"

Laughter. The orange-red glow of the branding stick hovered in her vision.

"Why do you think you was brought here? Gent like Darcy can ill afford an unfitting wife."

It could not be true. Mr. Darcy had offered for Elizabeth.

Of course, honorably, he had to. But to then sell her to these monsters. Lord Bee?

"He don' have love for you, miss. But stay still, and you can make a life for yourself in Bombay. Some of Lord Bee's misses make good for themselves. Be like a gentleman's wife."

The brand moved closer. Elizabeth screamed, kicking as she backed into a thick wall.

"This is 'bout when they start struggling, 'ent it, Lord Bee?"

The haunting glow of the brand illuminated a second figure. Tall. Broad shoulders and waist. She could make little of his features beyond a mustache, trimmed beard, and spectacles.

"Quiet." The man's voice resonated. It had a smooth quality that was almost pleasant. But the animal part of Elizabeth trembled. This was a predator, and worse, one who enjoyed hurting his prey.

Elizabeth screamed. "Help! Let me out!"

"Lord Bee, you hold her. Willow and I will do the marking."

Lord Bee grabbed her shoulders and spun her to face the wall. He smelled of bay leaves. Elizabeth flailed back with her elbow, connecting with something that made him loosen his grip for a second. She squirmed.

"Bart?" Lord Bee shoved Elizabeth forward. Her temple hit the wall, stunning her.

Searing pain. The smell of burning flesh mingled with bay leaves. Elizabeth screamed.

Agony.

Darkness.

Mist.

"If ye had'na run off, it would not be the cellar, miss."

No, Elizabeth could not think of that.

If Fitzwilliam had sent her away, why did he whisper to her now? Perhaps it was a trick of the mist. Like the smell of the sea and the sound of a pistol firing. Fitzwilliam's scent. The warmth of his arms.

All of it faraway.

The mist could not hide the anguish in Fitzwilliam's voice.

"Fitzwilliam? Why?" *Did you do this to me? Why? If you despised me so, I would have broken the engagement even if it destroyed me.*

"Why do I love you?" came his voice.

He sat cross-legged on the dock, a smile gracing his lips. Sunlight speckled his face. "I love you because of your kindness and wit. You make me smile. You make my heart light."

It made no sense. These were not the words of a man who cast away his inconvenient dalliance. Elizabeth leaned towards his voice, listening. "Why did you put me in that place?"

"You put yourself here. Elizabeth, my love, come back to me."

Elizabeth. Fitzwilliam. No barriers of propriety between them. That was the way of the mist.

But the mist was not real. How could she trust his words?

Fitzwilliam said, "I am waiting for you. Please, look at me. Let me know that you are here. I am waiting for you, and I love you so much."

Elizabeth wanted to believe him, but there was the matter of the brand. And the note. Elizabeth did not know Fitzwilliam's hand. Perhaps he had not written it?

Lady Catherine was the one who condemned her, threatened Charlotte, and sent Elizabeth off, without a chance to explain, in her carriage.

Lord Bee.

Elizabeth had thought the name a title. As Robin of the Wood was called a prince of thieves.

But what if Lord Bee was of the Ton? What if he and Lady Catherine were acquainted?

If so, how many others had Lady Catherine sent to this fate? How many more if Elizabeth did not return.

Elizabeth pulled the ether hand-over-hand on the tether, bringing herself and the small boat closer to shore. She dropped the excess rope in the boat's bottom and marveled at how the mist backed away as she came closer to him, her Fitzwilliam.

Birds chirped now.

In the cellar, she had heard the beat of footsteps above. Sometimes, Bart beat his wife and his son, and their screams echoed. He brutalized them and Elizabeth. The worst was the games.

"Do you want dinner?"

Flash of crooked teeth.

"A potato? A carrot? I cannot hear you."

Laughter.

"Water? What did you say? Ask me humbly, young miss."

When he left, Willow and the boy helped. The boy poured water through the slats, and his mother sometimes brought bread or stew.

It was never enough.

Here, the water was endless. She floated in it.

When she begged, she was given water from a glass. She grasped it, cool against her skin. Her throat, dry. Always dry.

Someone took her hand. Heart pounding, she looked down. Ghostly fingers wove between hers. Warmth. Here, her body was numb except for the heat of his fingers. Comforting.

"Lizzy, come back to me."

"Fitzwi—?"

"Her lips are moving! Oh, my dear, sweet daughter. Such a trial, our Lizzy. You will be a good girl and spare your mama's nerves."

What was Mama on about again? Mr. Collins? But Charlotte had married Mr. Collins. Or was it her hair? No, Elizabeth could not think about the hair. Or the rest of it. In the mist, she was whole.

Elizabeth ached. Her back. Her chest. Her head pounded. She wanted to let go again and drift. Drifting was safe. Comfortable.

The grip on her hand tightened. "Lizzy?"

Maybe if she ignored him, he would be quiet and let her drift. Except Elizabeth quite liked the feel of his hand in hers. Maybe he could join her in the mist. They could drift together.

Except his hand was too warm. Everything was

too warm. The duvet atop her. The pillow swallowing her cheek.

"Miss Elizabeth!"

"Quiet!" Her voice was hoarse. Too hoarse. "Thirsty."

"Lizzy?" Was that Jane? Elizabeth struggled to open her eyes.

"Water!" Mama screeched. "Where are the maids!"

"Yes." Jane again. "We will bring water. And broth. Will you eat for us?"

Mama was there. Jane. Mrs. Gardiner. Mr. Darcy. All of them.

Elizabeth lifted a hand to her hair.

Gone.

She ached.

Elizabeth squeezed her eyes shut. It had happened. The cellar. The brand. All of it. She was in her aunt and uncle's home. Before she shut her eyes, she had seen enough to recognize the room they always gave her when she visited.

They knew. Mr. Darcy was here, which meant he knew. And yet he stayed. He must care. Did he love her as he had said in the mist? How could he with all that had happened to her?

"Elizabeth?" Mr. Darcy's voice was gentle.

"Lizzy, you are awake; oh thank heaven and the Lord. Your father—!"

"I am right here, Letitia."

"Yes. We have not left your side, and neither has Mr. Darcy, a devoted gentleman, which considering your situation, our situation, is most fortunate."

Oh heavens, what if he was here out of pity? She was ruined. Not merely compromised, but ruined. If he married her, he would assume that burden. And she could not even be certain what they shared was love and not a dalliance followed by horror and shame.

"Let us allow our daughter some moments to settle herself, Letitia."

"We cannot leave Elizabeth unchaperoned."

"I believe we are well beyond the strictures of propriety," Mr. Bennet said.

Elizabeth's head pounded. "I am tired." She could not face them, nor Mr. Darcy now with everyone around.

In the mist, he had been Fitzwilliam. Now, he was Mr. Darcy, a man she had fallen in love with a lifetime ago.

"Yes. Of course." Mr. Darcy squeezed her hand. "I will stay close. I promise."

Mr. Darcy pulled his hand from hers, and Elizabeth was cold again. She wanted to reach for him. To say something. Tell him of her love, but would he consider her affection another burden?

The creak of an opening door, and a maid's voice, "Ma'am, broth, water, and some bread and fruits."

"May I stay?" Jane asked. She brushed her fingers over the fading bruise on Elizabeth's temple.

Biting her lip, Elizabeth gave a slight nod.

Jane sat.

When they were alone, Jane said, "You must be hungry, Lizzy, will you have a little food for me?"

Elizabeth opened her eyes, saw her sister's face, and sobbed.

"Oh Lizzy," Jane put her arms around Elizabeth and rocked her, like a child, until the tears became words.

"You can tell me, Lizzy," Jane said, holding Elizabeth to her breast. "All of it. When you are ready. You are safe now."

CHAPTER 20

Darcy was exhausted, having spent much of the evening pacing between his bed and the library, choosing and then discarding books he hoped would make Elizabeth smile. Nothing he said or did would change what happened to his beloved, and that he had not protected her weighed heavily.

Worse, Elizabeth did not trust him. She had sent him away. Darcy tried not to let that upset him. Of course, she wanted the comfort of her family. But she had to know how he felt about her.

The next morning, when Darcy and Richard arrived at the Gardiner's home, they were received in the drawing room by Mrs. Gardiner. A pillow, partially embroidered, sat on the chaise beside her.

Richard was impatient. "Has Miss Elizabeth said what happened to her?" Richard began. "Did she mention her abductors or Lord Braithwaite?"

Mrs. Gardiner said, "Elizabeth is fragile. She spoke with her sister but has sworn the young lady to secrecy, and Jane will not break Elizabeth's confidence.

"We have learned all we can from the others. But they are servants, and cannot alone bring their suit to the House of Lords. If Elizabeth saw something that will tie this to Lord Braithwaite, she must tell us."

"Richard!"

"We cannot allow Lord Braithwaite to escape justice for his crimes."

Darcy sighed. He agreed with his cousin, but his priority was Elizabeth's wellbeing. As much as he wanted Lord Braithwaite to suffer, he could not do it at Elizabeth's expense.

"May we see her?" Darcy asked.

"Provided you do not submit my niece to a barrage of questions." Mrs. Gardiner glared at Richard.

"We will not," Darcy said. He held out the book of poetry he had decided on the night before. "I had hoped to read to her."

Mrs. Gardiner nodded.

Richard said, "But if she wishes to speak...?"

"I want the ones who did this to her to suffer as well, Colonel." Mrs. Gardiner said. She took the pillow, pulling a needle from it and pinching it between her thumb and index finger. "Every stitch I make, I imagine it piercing this man's skin, the sharp pain, the blood, a pinprick at first, but then another and another until there is only red." She looked up. "But I will not punish him at Elizabeth's expense. Nor will I allow anyone else, however well intentioned, to cause her further harm."

Even Richard was silent.

Darcy said, "You have my word of honor. Your niece will be my wife, should she accept me, and I will protect her with my life. As I should have, not knowing the treachery in my own home."

Mrs. Gardiner nodded. "I trust you, Mr. Darcy. It is not a trust easily given. When Elizabeth is ready for company, it will be her pleasure to receive you." She put the pillow down and stood. "I will let Elizabeth know you wish to see her. Shall I call for refreshments?"

"Yes, thank you," Mr. Darcy said, resigning himself to wait.

AN HOUR LATER, MRS. GARDINER CAME INTO THE drawing room with Jane and Elizabeth Bennet in tow. Someone had worked miracles with Elizabeth's hair. It was still a boy's length, but the curls had been arranged beneath a lace cap in such a way that they framed her face in soft ringlets.

The rest of Elizabeth was drawn. Her cheekbones jutted and her eyes were a touch too large. They were dark, haunted pools.

Richard and Mr. Darcy stood, bowed.

"Miss Elizabeth," Mr. Darcy said, taking a step towards her.

Elizabeth looked down at her hands. They were bare, the nails short, cuticles and tips marked by tiny scars.

"Lizzy, it is Mr. Darcy," Jane said. "He has come to see you every day."

"Thank you," Elizabeth whispered.

Darcy swallowed. His stomach churned. "It was my pleasure, Miss Elizabeth." There was so much more to discuss. The abduction. Their future.

"You were Fitzwilliam, before."

Mrs. Gardiner coughed. Jane looked up at Darcy and Col. Fitzwilliam. "You saved my sister.

There are not enough words to express my gratitude. Our gratitude." Her eyes shone. Miss Jane Bennet had a beauty born of sincerity. Darcy doubted neither her words nor her abiding affection for Elizabeth.

The Drawing Room door opened, and Mrs. Bennet strode in. "Mr. Darcy! Colonel! I am appalled, must I say it, *appalled*, I was not here to receive you both. And Lizzy, looking so much brighter. Pleased to see you! Delighted! A finer gentleman I could never have imagined for my second-born, dear Lizzy."

Elizabeth squeezed her eyes shut.

Mrs. Gardiner went to her sister-in-law, took her by the arm and whispered something in her ear.

Mrs. Bennet gasped, and then, cocking her head said, "But her future——"

Mrs. Gardiner pinched Mrs. Bennet's arm.

"Ouch!"

Another whisper.

Mrs. Bennet sighed. "I had only wished to express my gratitude. My nerves being as they are, I am not my best, but there are no words to express what you have done for us. For our Lizzy! You saved our dearest Elizabeth from..." Another sigh. "I do not wish to imagine."

The door opened again, and Mr. Bennet, still in his morning dress, entered.

"Mr. Bennet! Receiving our sister's guests in such an appalling state!"

Elizabeth began to shake. She scratched at her fingers, whimpering. Jane pulled her close.

"Letitia! Be quiet!"

"Mr.—"

"Our daughter."

Mrs. Bennet turned. Clutched her hand to her throat. "Oh, Lizzy!" Her eyelids fluttered. She breathed through her teeth. "Our Elizabeth."

Mr. Bennet put an arm around his wife. "Come, it is just too many of us. Let us allow Elizabeth and her fiancé a moment. My sister will chaperone."

To Darcy's surprise, Mrs. Bennet nodded. "Yes. And you must choose a proper outfit, Mr. Bennet. We are not in our own home, my dear." She glanced back at her daughter and inhaled. "Elizabeth will be well, soon enough. She has always been headstrong, our Lizzy."

Mr. Bennet led his wife from the room.

Mr. Darcy turned to his cousin. "Perhaps Mr. Gardiner would like to be brought up to date on things. If Miss Elizabeth..." Darcy could not speak Lord Braithwaite's name nor make more than the barest allusion to the abduction, not now with Elizabeth so distressed. "I will tell you."

"Of course." Richard bowed.

Mrs. Gardiner took up her pillow and sat in a chair in the corner. Jane led Elizabeth to the sofa. Darcy sat on the chair at her side.

"How are you feeling?" Darcy asked.

"Well." Elizabeth looked down at her fingers, fiddling with them. The habit comforted him in its familiarity. Elizabeth often fiddled with things. Her fingers, bits of grass, her hair even. When otherwise calm or even dismissive, her fingers gave her away.

"I brought a book for you." Darcy said. He held out the slim volume of poetry.

Elizabeth said, "I cannot read now. The words swim in front of my eyes."

"Then I will read it to you." Darcy opened the book and began.

Mrs. Gardiner stitched and watched Mr. Darcy and her niece. While she feared the colonel might push Elizabeth too far, Mr. Darcy's devotion was plain. He had arrived every morning for three days to read poetry to Miss Elizabeth. Or sing. Or tell silly stories in obvious contrast to his serious demeanor.

A maid came in carrying tea, chocolate, warm

rolls and jam. He put a plate beside Darcy, who was too nervous to eat. He turned the page and continued to read, his gaze sneaking to Elizabeth. She was eating, at least. Slowly, she spread jam on a roll, bit and chewed. Jane encouraged Elizabeth to drink from the cup of steaming chocolate.

"Water?" Elizabeth asked.

"Yes, I will call for a maid." Jane rang the bell and consulted with the maid.

Darcy read.

The maid returned with a glass and pitcher. Mrs. Gardiner stitched her needlepoint, and Jane offered Elizabeth a second roll.

They passed perhaps ten minutes in amiable silence.

Darcy finished a fifth poem.

Elizabeth said, "You read to me, before."

Darcy smiled. "You remember. I also sang."

Elizabeth's nose wrinkled. It was the slightest motion, but in that moment, a sparkle came to her dark eyes and Darcy felt hope. Whatever had happened to Elizabeth, it had not broken her.

Darcy said, "I am not an accomplished singer."

"Lizzy sings beautifully," her sister said.

"Perhaps I cannot, now. My throat is always so dry."

"I will happily marry you, whether you sing or croak like a frog." Darcy smiled, and there was some relief at speaking of his feelings while both he and Elizabeth were sensate.

Elizabeth said, "If you do not wish to marry me, I will not insist upon the proposal."

"Lizzy," Jane cut in. "Of course, Mr. Darcy wishes to marry you! He saved you from those horrible men. And he has been here every day."

"I will be an embarrassment. My hair." She lifted her hand to her shorn locks.

"I do not wish to marry you for your hair, Miss Elizabeth."

"I am not myself." Elizabeth waved a hand at her face, the fading bruises on her temple, the scratches on her fingers. "Loud noises make me flinch. Too many people, even my own family; I cannot—" She sobbed. "I want to forget all of it. Erase it."

"I cannot change what has happened to you. But none of this has changed my affection. I love you." Mr. Darcy declared. "Your hair will grow and your bruises will heal."

"And his brand?"

"Lizzy!"

"He ought to know."

"I know. There were others. They were found on the boat where those men were taking you."

"How many?"

"Four."

Elizabeth bowed her head. Tears shone in her lashes.

"Bart said I was to go to India. Lord Bee," Elizabeth scratched her fingers. Fiddling. "He—"

"What did he do?" Darcy reached out, covered her hands in his. "If he has—" Acid rose in Darcy's throat. Forget the Council of Lords. Darcy would find Lord Braithwaite and rend him limb from limb. But he had to stay calm for Elizabeth's sake. What if she assumed he was angry with her, and not Lord Braithwaite? He breathed in. "You can tell me. If you wish. Whatever happened, it changes nothing."

"He held me. Bart branded me, but Lord Bee —!" Elizabeth turned her palm upward and squeezed his hand. "He smelled of bay leaves. And his voice." She swallowed. "I bet he sings like an angel."

Lucifer, more like.

"Whatever mark he put on your skin, your name is burned on my heart. He cannot have you because you are mine. As I am yours. Body and soul."

"Fitzwilliam—!" Her voice caught.

"I want to grow old with you. Long from now, we will have wrinkles and warts, and I will love you just the same."

Silence. Elizabeth's shoulders shook. She looked up, eyes shining, her lips formed in a tremulous smile. "You believe this will make me feel better? I can trade bruises for warts?"

"Do not overlook the wrinkles," Darcy laughed. "And I will be paunchy and with gray hair and warts, and despite these failings, you will love me still."

"Bart, Lord Bee's man, said you had sent me away. He showed me a note."

"It was not me."

"I know."

A note, written in an approximation of his hand. Darcy had not wanted to believe, even now, his aunt had been involved in Elizabeth's abduction, but he could not hide from the truth.

"I love you."

"You said that."

"And I am saying it again. And again." Darcy laughed.

"Aunt Amelia?" Jane stood, suddenly, and walked with her back towards them to the chair where her aunt sat, dutifully focused on her stitching.

Neither Darcy nor Elizabeth noticed. Darcy leaned off the chair and knelt in front of Elizabeth, their hands still clasped.

"I always vowed to marry for love," Elizabeth said. "But when Mr. Collins found us, I feared you would feel trapped and despise me. In the soil of misunderstanding, love would die."

"The only misunderstanding was that I did not declare myself sooner. Will you forgive me?"

"I suppose I must. I am not as I was though."

"Then I will love you as you are, so long as you promise me the same."

Darcy looked up. Elizabeth lowered her lips, and they kissed.

A soft kiss. Promise rather than passion.

"I promise," Elizabeth agreed.

EPILOGUE

"It is not enough." Richard pressed his index fingers at the bridge of his nose. He and Mr. Darcy stood in Mr. Gardiner's study with Mr. Gardiner and Mr. Bennet. Mr. Gardiner sat at his desk with Mr. Bennet in a chair on the opposite side. Two glasses of port sat atop it, the one closest to Mr. Bennet half-empty.

"Elizabeth recognizes his scent and his voice," Darcy argued.

"But Miss Elizabeth did not see him."

"He held her down for the brand. And they found the other abducted women on Lord Braithwaite's boat."

"Which his solicitor is blaming on the captain who will hang on Friday." Richard sighed. "Even if

Elizabeth had seen Lord Braithwaite's face, it would still be her word against his, and he is powerful. A favorite of the Regent's."

While some gentlemen had strong opinions about Prinny, Darcy did not much think of the Prince Regent. London was far from Derbyshire, and Darcy preferred his life in the country. He also despised gossip, which in his experience, gentlemen enjoyed at least as much as ladies did.

"And the captain. Will he not turn on Lord Braithwaite to save his skin?"

"The captain confessed."

"What?"

Richard laughed, a bitter sound. "A man will confess to anything, when the right force is applied."

"So we have nothing." How could they tell Elizabeth the man who had abducted and nearly sold her to a depraved gentleman across the sea with funds to force an unwilling wife?

Mr. Gardiner reached into the bottom drawer of his desk and took out two more glasses. "There must be something we can do, Colonel."

"Where is he? I can demand honor for what he did to my fiancée. I will write the letter this evening."

"And if Lord Braithwaite kills you, Darcy? What of Elizabeth then? Even if you win, Prinny might exact some retaliation. Or others in court."

"We need to prove Lord Braithwaite is responsible," Mr. Gardiner said. "This was not a matter of one captain and one ship. These women were abducted, hidden, branded and sent for transport to India and perhaps other colonies. These steps will leave evidence. I will look on the shipping side."

Richard said, "Good. Lord Braithwaite has his lands and habits. And if he visited Miss Elizabeth, he likely visited the others he abducted. Not to mention the matter of the branding. Had he not abducted Elizabeth, he would continue to operate with impunity, but we will see to it he can do this to no other woman."

How many other young women had Lord Braithwaite already kidnapped and sold into bondage?

Mr. Bennet said, "I have some acquaintances in the Home Office who might give me some information."

Richard took a sip of his port. "If we can get information about Lord Braithwaite's whereabouts this past year, we will then be able to ask about missing or 'runaway' servants and see if we cannot establish a pattern. With all of our efforts, we will get the information we need, and make certain Lord Braithwaite does not escape justice again."

All agreed.

Darcy said, "And I will speak with my aunt. Lady Catherine and Lord Braithwaite are acquainted."

How long had Aunt Catherine known about him? Darcy could only pray his aunt had not known the extent of Lord Braithwaite's crimes. If she had, she was a monster.

Mr. Bennet narrowed his eyes. "Lady Catherine de Bourgh?"

Darcy nodded.

"Lady Catherine sent Elizabeth away, most cruelly. She is involved, then?"

Darcy wanted to prevaricate. Say he had no evidence of his aunt's involvement, but he could not deny his own instincts. Lady Catherine was kind to those whose status she felt worthy or, conversely, those who honored her every thought as the highest wisdom. Elizabeth was neither of those things, and her compromise with Darcy had interfered in Lady Catherine's plans.

"There is another matter, Mr. Bennet," Mr.

Darcy said. "If we may speak together, in private, about your daughter."

"Jane speaks highly of you."

"I do not wish to marry Jane—Miss Bennet! I mean, she is a lovely woman, it is only my fondness for Miss Elizabeth—"

Mr. Bennet laughed. The expression wrinkled well-worn laugh lines around his eyes and lips. "I assume Lizzy is agreeable to your proposal."

"Yes."

"Then you have my blessing."

"Congratulations, Fitzwilliam." Richard clapped his cousin, a bit too vigorously, on the back. "I wish you both the best of happiness."

Darcy smiled. It was a beginning, at the least.

"Mrs. Bennet will wish to have some say in the wedding preparations. And selfishly, I hope you do not take our Lizzy away from us too soon."

Darcy nodded. Elizabeth was still recovering from her ordeal. As much as Darcy wanted to marry her and live as husband and wife, she needed her family, especially her sister Jane, as she returned to herself. Also, a wedding done in too much haste showed shame. Elizabeth deserved better than that.

"You live in Hertfordshire?"

Mr. Bennet nodded. "Near the village of Meryton. There are some estates, the closest being Netherfield Hall, which are to let for a season."

"Then I shall take it." Darcy decided. As much as he knew Elizabeth, with her love of walking and natural beauty, would love Pemberley, he had a lifetime to show her the beauty of his... no, *their*, home.

Small steps.

Mr. Bennet stood. Bowed. "For all you have done for Lizzy, I could not be prouder to bring a gentleman into our family. Though I warn you, a lesser gentleman might find it overwhelming." That hint of a smile, again. "It is fortunate you are not a lesser gentleman."

"I shall strive to overcome," Darcy said.

Richard laughed. "Darcy is nothing if not the striving sort."

Darcy glared at his cousin. "What is it you mean by that statement?"

"Nothing." Richard's lips twitched. "Nothing at all. Perhaps you should share the good news with Miss Elizabeth?"

Yes. He would tell Elizabeth all of it, including his decision to spend the autumn at Netherfield or whatever local estate was within easy walking, or at the worst, horseback distance.

Before Darcy left, he visited Elizabeth again.

She sat in the garden, his book of poetry in her lap. The book was closed, and Elizabeth's ungloved fingers rested on the leather cover.

"Miss Elizabeth?" Darcy bowed.

Elizabeth turned her head to him and smiled.

"May I sit?" He gestured to the empty section of bench. The garden was small, shielded from the noisy street by a tall, stone wall. Inside was mostly flowers and shrubbery arranged in neat rows around a central courtyard where two benches sat opposite each other.

Elizabeth smiled. "Please."

Darcy sat and took her hand. "I spoke with Mr. Bennet."

"I trust he had no objections to your proposal."

"He wishes you happy."

Elizabeth said, "I will be."

"You will. Mr. Bennet says there is an estate to lease near you, a Netherfield Hall. Shall we marry near your home?"

"But you live in Derbyshire."

"Yes. But I have business in Town these next few months, and it will be best for you to be near your family, at least for a while. If that is something you would like."

Elizabeth's eyes shone. "You would do that, for me?"

"I would do anything for you, Miss Elizabeth."

"In the mist, we were Elizabeth and Fitzwilliam."

"The mist?"

"Where you called me from. When I was... gone... Is Fitzwilliam appropriate?"

"You can call me whatever you like."

Elizabeth's dark eyes twinkled, and Darcy glimpsed the humor that had drawn him to her such a short and long time ago. "Fitzy then?"

"Not Fitzy."

"Willy?"

"This is hardly fair."

"You have no nickname for me?"

"Beloved."

"That is not a nickname."

"It is an endearment." With his index finger, Darcy flicked the tip of her nose.

Elizabeth wrinkled it. "Stop that."

"Stop what, beloved?"

"Fitzy—!"

"If you call me Fitzy again, I shall take drastic measures."

"Will I enjoy them?"

Darcy touched Elizabeth's jaw with his finger-tips, gently turning her head towards him. "Per-haps." It was a joy to see the light in her eyes as she teased him. He had feared her lost, but though she was still hurting, she had not shattered. She had returned to him. He would be forever grateful for that gift, for her.

Elizabeth smiled. "Fitzy. Fitzy-witzy!"

"What did you say?"

"Fit—!"

Darcy kissed her, passion and promise. Her lips parted, welcoming, as she kissed him back. They drifted together, lost in each other's warmth.

"Lizzy! Where are you? Jane said you wished to read, alone, but— Oh!"

Elizabeth pulled away. "Mama!"

"Mr. Darcy!"

"We are to be married."

"You are not married yet, Lizzy. Though Mr. Bennet says Mr. Darcy is to let Netherfield Park! Oh, Mr. Darcy, do hold a ball or two. Lizzy has four sisters who have most amicable dispositions and are so handsome. You have met our Jane. It would be quite an easement for my nerves to see them all wed, you understand."

Darcy had come to a thorough understanding

of Mrs. Bennet's nerves in the time they had waited by Elizabeth's bedside.

"Mama, Mr. Darcy was just finishing his proposal."

"You said yes, I pray!"

"Yes, Mama."

"Good. Excellent. Mrs. Lucas will be at all ends when she hears you are to marry such a fine, handsome, and wealthy gentleman. My sister, Mrs. Phillips, has spoken so fondly of Pemberley. She went north three summers back, and had intended to tour Derbyshire again this summer, though I suppose that visit will be put on hold until you return."

Elizabeth lifted her shawl from where it had fallen behind her on the bench. Though the air was warm, she often complained of a chill now, dressing in thick stockings, sleeves and a shawl. "Mama, I believe Mr. Darcy must take his leave."

"Yes, and we shall have the banns announced next Sunday."

"I had intended Elizabeth and me to wed by Special License."

Mrs. Bennet's eyes widened. "Special License. How grand! A fine gentleman, whatever nonsense Mr. Collins wrote of your ruining my daughter. No such talk will happen in our house. Compromise indeed! For shame! I knew upon laying eyes on you, Mr. Darcy, that you were a gentleman of excellent character. Such a fine gentleman."

Elizabeth stood. "Thank you, Mr. Darcy. I am honored at your proposal, and I accept."

"Of course she accepts! Lizzy would not be such a fool to say nay to a fine catch a second time!"

Elizabeth sighed.

Mr. Darcy smiled, renewed with the hope and joy of what lay ahead with Miss Elizabeth Bennet, nay, Mrs. Elizabeth Darcy, his beloved wife.

The End.

Thank you for reading!

I hope you enjoyed reading this book as much as I loved writing it! If so, you can learn more about my books, read free chapters, and get email updates at violetkingauthor.com. There is a sample of one of my other books, An Unsuitable Governess, in the next chapter if you'd like a taste.

Lastly, if you enjoyed this book and have a 3-minutes to leave a quick review, I cannot thank you enough! Reviews are how readers decide if they are ready to give a new author a try. For indie authors like me, having readers share their honest views about my books with other readers is a precious gift.

Thank you again so much for reading!

All the best,

Violet

AN UNSUITABLE GOVERNESS

Sparks fly when Miss Elizabeth Bennet takes work as a governess at Pemberley.

Will deceptions, highwaymen, and a rambunctious eleven-year-old girl bring Elizabeth and Mr. Darcy together or tear them apart?

After rejecting Mr. Collins proposal, Miss Elizabeth Bennet assumes the persona of a widow and goes to Lambton to find work. But when she befriends Mr. Darcy's half-sister Rose and becomes her governess, she must contend with Mr. Darcy, a man she wishes to despise, and Col. Richard Fitzwilliam, a man she wants to love but cannot.

With Rose's help, will Elizabeth find the strength to follow her heart?

Mr. Fitzwilliam Darcy would sooner face bandits than return to Pemberley and deal with his stepmother -- alas, he must do both. And when he discovers Miss Elizabeth Bennet in his home, serving as governess to his half-sister Rose, things go from bad to worse. Col. Fitzwilliam is falling for her. Mr. Darcy is too -- or would be, if Miss Elizabeth were at all suitable. Will Mr. Darcy stop denying his heart my before his cousin steals Elizabeth's?

Find out in **An Unsuitable Governess**, a standalone Pride and Prejudice novel of 64,000 words.

Warning! This book contains: one not at all wicked stepmother, one 100% wicked band of highwaymen, one rambunctious eleven-year-old, one deceptive governess with a heart of gold, one love-stricken colonel, one handsome gentleman in denial of his true feelings, one found treasure, and two happily ever afters to set your heart aflutter.

Chapter 1

Beneath a gray and weeping sky, a Royal Mail stagecoach trundled north towards Derbyshire. Miss

Elizabeth Bennet wished to pretend it was all a grand adventure, but three days being jounced about until her muscles and teeth ached and three nights in tiny coaching inn rooms with the thin, ill-tempered maid Mrs. Gardiner had insisted Elizabeth bring as a chaperone, had robbed Elizabeth of her sense of wonder. Her eyelids were stiff, her hair itched, and she stank.

Across from Elizabeth sat a white-haired, plump woman with spectacles on her nose and a book in her lap. She traced the text with her index finger as she read, pausing occasionally to take a sip from her hip flask or glance out the window at the patchwork fields.

Elizabeth glanced over at her, and then, fearing rudeness, turned her attention back to the pillow on her lap. Gripping the needle between her thumb and forefinger, she sewed. Beside her on the bench, the maid turned chaperone, Adelaide, slept with her head tipped back, mouth parted and snoring like an angry cricket.

"Is it your first time in a public coach?" the woman across from her asked.

Was it so obvious? Elizabeth stabbed the needle into the pillow. "Yes."

"It is not so terrible." The woman closed her

book and placed it on the bench beside her. She lifted her hip flask and took a sip. "Have you and your... friend," she glanced at Adelaide. "Come up all the way from London?"

Elizabeth nodded.

"Long journey. You must be exhausted." The woman held out her hip flask. "Have a taste. It will warm your bones."

Elizabeth hesitated. She was not in the habit of accepting refreshments from strangers. "What is it?"

"My special mix for long trips. Go on, then."

Elizabeth glanced over at Adelaide, but the maid did not stir. A fine protector. But Elizabeth was thirsty, and she appreciated the offer of friendship. She took the flask and sipped cautiously.

Liquid fire burned down her throat. Elizabeth coughed, blinking rapidly.

The old woman chuckled. "My specialty. Tea with a touch of lavender and a healthy dollop of gin."

"It is bracing," Elizabeth said, handing the flask back. Now that the initial burn had passed, the drink had warmed her, or at least distracted her from the chill, damp air and Elizabeth's own nerves.

"Are you visiting family up north?"

"In Lambton. And I am hoping to find work as a governess or a lady's companion."

Elizabeth's hands shook. She was really doing this, putting her life and her prospects behind her and seeking work.

After rejecting Mr. Collins' proposal, life at Longbourn had become intolerable. If her aunt and uncle had not visited and yielded to Elizabeth's entreaties to take her with them to Town, she might have buckled, not to Mr. Collins, who had already wed Charlotte, but to another fool with a good income whom Elizabeth did not admire.

No, it was better she left. The life of a governess was uncertain, and for many unhappy, but if Elizabeth could not marry for love, she would not marry at all. And if she was not to marry, then she needed to provide for herself. She refused to be a burden to her family.

"Lambton! Why, that is my destination. My niece is with child, and I wished to give her some aid, what with her husband being away with Wellington's men. Have you any brothers on the front? We might pray, together."

Elizabeth was touched. "I have no brothers, but if you wish to pray..." Elizabeth had prayed enough this past month for guidance or at least comfort. Perhaps God had guided her here.

"In a bit, perhaps. You are not so fond of embroidery, are you, Miss—?"

Elizabeth bit the inside of her cheek. As tired and sore as she was from the days of travel, once she left this coach, her future became even more uncertain. "Elizabeth," she said.

The maid snorted and rubbed her hand over her cheek. Drool glistened from the corner of her mouth.

"Elizabeth Ben—" No. Once she left this coach, Miss Elizabeth Bennet would disappear. Best to begin now.

"Mrs. Elizabeth Wilson," Elizabeth declared. Wilson was her aunt's maiden name and the one she had chosen to begin her new life.

The old woman's eyebrow twitched. "Mrs. Wilson," she said, smiling with one missing tooth. "Evelyn. Mrs. Evelyn Johnson. It is a pleasure to meet you."

The carriage jerked.

"Huh?" Adelaide rubbed her eyes. The carriage jerked again. Elizabeth gripped the seat as ahead, the driver, astride one of the heavy draft horses, pulled back on the reins, shouting. The horses turned left, slowing beside a carriage which appeared to have tipped onto its side. The horses were gone.

"Goodness! I had not believed the rumors!" Mrs. Johnson exclaimed.

"Rumors?"

"Highwaymen."

Elizabeth swallowed. She peered out the side window. A footman hopped down from the coach. He held a coach gun in hand as he approached the downed carriage.

Adelaide said, "Cor! Mrs. Gardiner said no such thing of us being robbed."

"Perhaps there was an accident," Elizabeth suggested.

"Humph! What accident run off with the horses?"

Adelaide made an excellent point.

The footman returned, shaking his head as he walked back. He spoke briefly to the driver and then walked towards the back of the coach. Elizabeth stood.

"What are you doing?" Adelaide said as Elizabeth opened the stagecoach door.

"Finding out what is going on," Elizabeth said. A cold wind swept into the carriage. "Excuse me,"

Elizabeth shouted to the footman as he passed. "What happened?"

"Nothing to concern yourself with, Miss."

"Was anyone hurt?"

"No. It is empty."

An empty carriage, no horses, and rumors of highwaymen. Elizabeth shivered.

"We'll be on our way again, Miss, if you would like to get settled in."

Elizabeth thanked him and pulled the door shut.

"Cor," Adelaide said again as the coach rumbled forward. "They gon' report it at the next station?"

"I suppose," Elizabeth said, seating herself again on the bench. As the driver guided the horses, Elizabeth reached up to the shawl around her shoulders and clasped it around her.

Mrs. Johnson took another swig from her flask. "Lambton is a quiet town. You were looking for work as a governess, you said?"

Elizabeth nodded. Thoughts of the empty carriage had driven away fears about her future employment.

"Try the Darcy house," Mrs. Johnson advised, holding the flask out again.

"Darcy?" It could not be the same odious Darcy who had mocked her and then danced with her with all the warmth of a plasterwork. Though Jane, or perhaps their mother, had mentioned Mr. Darcy's estate was in the North.

"At Pemberley. The youngest Darcy girl has been quite the terror since their father's passing, my niece says. She is just eleven and since last summer has driven away three young governesses on her own."

Pemberley. That was the name of Mr. Darcy's estate. Elizabeth had little doubt Mr. Darcy's sister was a terror. She would be following in the family tradition.

"Thank you," Elizabeth said, resolving to find work elsewhere. Highwaymen. Monster children, and now this.

"I would not have suggested it, love, but you were so fierce just then with the footman." Mrs. Johnson held the flask out again, and Elizabeth took it. Mrs. Elizabeth Wilson needed a taste of courage.

Thank you for reading!

I hope you enjoyed reading this book as much as I loved writing it! If so, you can read more of this book, learn more about my books for free online, and get email updates at violetkingauthor.com.

Lastly, if you enjoyed this book and have a 3-minutes to leave a quick review, I cannot thank you enough! Reviews are how readers decide if they are ready to give a new author a try. For indie authors like me, having readers share their honest views about my books with other readers is a precious gift.

Thank you again so much for reading!

All the best,

Violet

SPECIAL THANK YOU

First I give thanks to God and my mom for supporting me even on my grumpiest writing days. Next, a HUGE THANK YOU to Elizabeth Ann West who encouraged me to try my hand at writing in the world of Pride and Prejudice. Also, so much love and gratitude to the whole writing productivity gang, including Pat, Mr. Sparkle, Susannah, Dana, Cora, Echo, and my admin wench, Bella who kept me getting those words on the page with gold stars galore!

I also deeply want to thank Donna, my editor, who caught some really big mistakes on my part and fixed them!

I am thankful to the wonderful readers and reviewers on my membership site who left comments, including, Jansfamily4, Shelby07, maeseaview, Mrs_SP9, justJan, cekepler, Shelby07, HappyLizzy and wonderful readers on FFnet Graciela and NS2301 who let me know about an important issue in Chapter 9, and countless others who encouraged me and let me know when my Regency (and overall story) went awry, you have my heartfelt gratitude.

And **I am wildly grateful to my ARC team** who have generously read this book in advance and given their honest reviews of my work. You are all angels in human form!

ABOUT THE AUTHOR

Violet King is a Pennsylvania native who loves reading and writing Regency romance. She had some Pride and Prejudice plot bunnies that wouldn't leave her be, so she started writing her first JAFF in 2018. Her first book, Mr. Darcy's Cipher, is inspired by her interest in history and the desire to write about a smart, savvy heroine who saves her country while falling in love.

Violet's other interests include drawing and painting, trying specialty teas (she lived in Japan for a few years and is especially picky about Jasmines and Greens,) cuddling her cats, karaoke, and reading, reading, reading! You can learn more about her books and sign up for her newsletter at violetkingauthor.com.